Eight Stories

EIGHT STORIES

Tales of War and Loss

ERICH MARIA REMARQUE

Introduction by

MARIA TATAR *and* **LARRY WOLFF**

WASHINGTON MEWS BOOKS
An Imprint of
NEW YORK UNIVERSITY PRESS
New York

WASHINGTON MEWS BOOKS
An Imprint of
NEW YORK UNIVERSITY PRESS
New York
www.nyupress.org | © 2018 by New York University | All rights reserved

Book designed and typeset by Charles B. Hames

Library of Congress Cataloging-in-Publication Data
Names: Remarque, Erich Maria, 1898–1970 author. |
Tatar, Maria, 1945– author of introduction. | Wolff, Larry author of introduction.
Title: Eight stories : tales of war and loss / Erich Maria Remarque ;
introduction by Maria Tatar and Larry Wolff.
Description: New York : Washington Mews Books, 2018. |
Seven of the eight short stories in this collection were originally published
in Collier's magazine. The eighth story, Dreamt Last Night, was published in
Redbook magazine. | Includes bibliographical references and index. Identifiers:
LCCN 2017054994 | ISBN 9781479824854 (cl : alk. paper) |
ISBN 9781479888092 (pb : alk. paper)
Classification: LCC PT2635.E68 A2 2018 | DDC 833/.912—dc23
LC record available at https://lccn.loc.gov/2017054994

CONTENTS

A NOTE ON THE TEXT

Seven of the eight short stories in this collection were originally published in *Collier's* magazine. The eighth story, "I Dreamt Last Night," was published in *Redbook Magazine.* Translators were not credited alongside Remarque's byline with the stories, and the copyright record for the individual stories stated that the translator was anonymous and for hire. Likely translators for the stories are either A. W. Wheen, who translated many of Remarque's works from German to English, including *All Quiet on the Western Front,* or Denver Lindley, who also translated a number of Remarque's novels and who worked as an editor at *Collier's* beginning in 1927.

ORIGINAL PUBLICATION DATES
OF SELECTED STORIES

"The Enemy," *Collier's National Weekly,* March 29, 1930

"Silence," *Collier's National Weekly,* June 28, 1930

"Where Karl Had Fought," *Collier's National Weekly,*
August 23, 1930

"Josef's Wife," *Collier's National Weekly,* November 21, 1931

"Annette's Love Story," *Collier's National Weekly,*
November 28, 1931

"The Strange Fate of Johann Bartok," *Collier's National Weekly,*
December 5, 1931

"On the Road," *Collier's National Weekly,* January 20, 1934

"I Dreamt Last Night," *Redbook Magazine,* December 1, 1934

REMARQUE AT *COLLIER'S*

Writing about War for the American Public in the 1930s

MARIA TATAR, *Harvard University*
LARRY WOLFF, *New York University*

In 1945 Erich Maria Remarque told a *New York Times* reporter that he was no longer a German: "For I do not think in German nor feel German, nor talk German. Even when I dream it is about America, and when I swear, it is in American."[1] He had left Germany for Switzerland in 1933, just a day before Adolf Hitler was named chancellor. Stripped of German citizenship in 1938, Remarque had already made a new home for himself in the Swiss village of Porto Ronco near Locarno. A year later, together with his ex-wife Ilse Sambona (the two had divorced in 1930), he sailed to the United States on the *Queen Mary*. War broke out while they were at sea, and the ship was led to port by a British cruiser. Remarque became a naturalized citizen of the United States in 1947.

Remarque's name is so closely associated with the novel *All Quiet on the Western Front* (the book's title referred ironically to a recurring phrase in the Kaiser's wartime communiqués) that it is easy to forget how his literary career extended into and beyond the 1930s and that he became something of a celebrity writer in the United States. Less reclusive than one might expect from an author who captured the existential distress of an entire generation, he consorted with an international Hollywood set that included Marlene Dietrich, Charlie Chaplin, Greta Garbo, Luise Rainer, Douglas Sirk, and Paulette Goddard (who later became his second wife). Still, the *New York Times* reported in Remarque's obituary that the reputation as a "nightclubber" and frequent appearances at the Stork Club and at 21 did not really mark him as a "carouser" so much as "a night owl with a taste for fine foods and memorable champagne."[2]

Los Angeles, with its colony of German exiles, seemed like a natural second home for Remarque, who turned his melancholy good looks and European sophistication to good account. "Refugees from Hitler arrived in droves," the actor David Niven recalled. "When Erich Maria Remarque was not wrapped around Marlene Dietrich or other local beauties, he acted as a sort of liaison officer."[3] But Remarque never felt comfortable in Los Angeles, an urban setting with none of the urbanity he associated with cities like Berlin, Paris, or New York. A *flaneur* by nature, Remarque feared that he might be arrested for loitering while taking walks in Beverly Hills, a place with no tolerance for leisurely strolls driven by the human instinct to observe others and take in (even suburban) sights. He was more invested in the other coast, and soon combined the glamour of Hollywood with the cosmopolitan pleasures of New York City night life. "New York! That really is a city without the melancholy and oppressive charm of the past! An explosion of life! The future!"[4]

It did not help that the community of German refugee writers in Los Angeles had failed to embrace Remarque as one of their own. Was it professional jealousy? Intellectual snobbery? Remarque had, after all, attained a degree of international celebrity and commercial success through the publication of *All Quiet on the Western Front* that seemed to outdo Thomas Mann and Bertolt Brecht, luminaries in the German-speaking world—even if Mann was the writer who had secured the Nobel Prize. "Remarque has made it clear he 'hates' me," Thomas Mann confided in his diary. "His boorish behavior had made that clear before."[5] It is hard to imagine that someone whose behavior you consider "boorish" would reciprocate with warmth. In fact, part of the boorish behavior may well have been motivated by Mann's disdain for a writer

lacking his own trademark complexity, sophistication, and depth. Brecht was no less disparaging, of-
fended by a compatriot who showed up at events
with a "Hollywood Mexican star" on his arm and
who wore tailored tuxedos (a cardinal sin in the
playwright's book). "His face lacks something,
probably a monocle," he added derisively, reveal-
ing just how deeply his contempt for the novelist
ran, despite the fact that Remarque was in so many
ways a kindred spirit, a writer whose books—
along with works by Thomas Mann, Maxim Gorky,
James Joyce, Heinrich Mann, and Brecht himself—
had been tossed by the Nazis into bonfires set at
the Opernplatz in Berlin on May 10, 1933.[6]

Erich Paul Remark was born in the German city
Osnabrück in 1898. He later reverted to the original French spelling of his last name (with the hope
of dissociating himself from the extravagances of
the first novel he had written, the title of which he
said he would refuse to divulge, "even under torture") and added the middle name Maria, most

likely as a double homage to his mother and to the poet Rainer Maria Rilke.[7] Conscripted into the German army at age eighteen in 1917, he was moved toward the Western front and served in a trench unit in Belgium based somewhere between the town of Thourout and the forest of Houthulst. Wounded during the Battle of Flanders that same year, he spent the last two years of the war in a German army hospital. In the postwar period he took a range of jobs, in advertising (writing copy) and in sales (specializing in monuments and tombstones). He also worked, with limited success, as a journalist, teacher, and editor.

Remarque's second novel, *All Quiet on the Western Front*, was written in 1927 and did not immediately find a publisher. But once the *Vossische Zeitung* serialized the work to great acclaim in 1928, it was picked up by the distinguished publishing house Ullstein and became an instant bestseller, despite brisk competition from a wave of war novels appearing in the late 1920s. Remarque's novel captured the imagination not just of war veterans, but also of an entire civilian population. Its appeal crossed national boundaries and the volume was quickly translated into dozens of languages, with remarkably strong sales continuing over the decades. In America the book became a standard feature of high school curricula and summer reading assignments.

≈

All Quiet on the Western Front has been called the greatest anti-war novel of all time, and, more than other war novels published in that year—most famously Hemingway's *A Farewell to Arms* and Frederic Manning's *The Middle Parts of Fortune*—it offers a passionate indictment of the horrors of combat, showing how the machinery of war destroys bodies, shatters skulls, tears limbs from torsos, and rips away flesh to expose vital organs. Less confrontational than Ernst Friedrich's photo album *War against War!* (1924), with its chilling photographs of soldiers on battlefields and wounded veterans back home, *All Quiet on the Western Front* gave its readers interiority and intimacy as only fiction can, relaying the lived experience that silenced real-life veterans of that war (the loss of the storytelling instinct in the period following World War I was of deep concern to Walter Benjamin in his 1936 meditation on the storyteller).[8] It also revealed how the fog of war is both world-shattering and word-shattering, making it impossible to build meaning and sense, and consequently producing a cascading series of crises ranging from the linguistic to the existential.

What emerged from Remarque's war novel was a new aesthetic register that moved in the mode of the grotesque, valuing fragmentation and deformation in its representational practices. It was a register uncannily anticipated by the German Expressionists, the French Fauves, and the Italian Futurists, along with the Cubists. "The broken world that emerged from the carnage seemed to have made prophets of the Cubists," Simon Schama writes, in an effort to explain how the prewar avant-garde provided an aesthetic script for the era following World War I.[9] German painters like Franz Marc affirmed that there was a certain "artistic logic" to painting a Cubist work like his *Tierschicksale* "*before* the war, rather than their being stupid reminiscences *after* the war."[10] Remarque's narrative style may in fact be seen as a belated form of literary modernism, less conventional than most critics have held.

The authorization of grotesque disfiguration—of an artistic strategy that Marc called both "horrifying and moving"—was also part of a program that endorsed affective engagement and sympathetic identification, perhaps in a bid to compensate for unspeakable physical injuries and the loss of bodily integrity. Bodies dead, injured, and mutilated "magnetically" draw forth our sympathy, as Sarah Cole has pointed out, and encounters with the dead are accompanied by an urge to memorialize, to invest the dead with a story.[11] The instinct to memorialize becomes evident when the novel's hero, Paul Bäumer, almost as a reflex, grabs a pencil from the pocket of the Frenchman he has just killed and declares his intention to write a letter to the man's wife. The author of *All Quiet on the Western Front* engages in the same form of memory work by writing the story of a combatant shot just before the war ends, on a day when, in a final ironic twist, all is said to be "quiet."

By 1930, Remarque had sold over a million copies of his book in Germany, and two million elsewhere, and his fame quickly spread to the United States, where the Hollywood dream factory worked its magic to turn the nightmarish events in Remarque's novel into a gripping film, directed by Lewis Milestone and released in 1930. When the film was shown in Berlin, the screening was disrupted by a "Dr. Goebbels" and three hundred of his followers, as the *New York Times* reported a day later on December 7, 1930.[12] "Organized booing, catcalling, throwing malodorous bombs and releasing white mice in the theatre"—this was the reaction to a film thought to betray veterans of the war by taking a pacifist stand and promoting a form of international solidarity that crossed national lines.

Remarque, in the meantime, had moved on, if not yet from Berlin, then at least with his writing. Working on *All Quiet on the Western Front*, he had, both instinctively and intellectually, set out to write "an anti-war novel," one that ended with the narrator's death, despite pleas from his publisher to let Paul Bäumer survive and live on in sequels. He believed that a rewrite culminating in the "triumph of survival" would have betrayed the pacifist spirit of the work and produced something akin to "an adventure yarn," one stripped of the tragic pathos in the original work.

In later years, Remarque found himself less reluctant to experiment with narratives about the "triumph of survival," though, tellingly, he wrote about the dark side to survival—the challenges of returning from war and experiencing the shock waves of civilian life. If *All Quiet on the Western Front* gave readers scenes of horrific trench warfare and explosive scenes of human carnage, Remarque's later work, most notably the novel *The Way Back*, tells about how new pathologies emerged in the postwar era—shell shock, battle fatigue, and war neurosis most obviously, but also all kinds of other symptoms, including perverse nostalgia for the combat zone, a need to reenact military maneuvers, and in general an inability to process the horrors of war and a lack of opportunity to talk about them.

Remarque himself discovered his own unique way back through writing, giving us accounts not only of his own war experiences, but also those of his comrades in arms. *All Quiet on the Western Front* had been a mix of autobiographical experience and stories told by fellow soldiers, as the author once explained in an interview. Even after the war, Remarque continued to document combat memories through the consciousness of veterans returning from war and finding themselves in emotional distress—physically impaired, socially dislocated, and psychologically ill-equipped to manage a life forever disrupted by the war experience. These became the characters featured in the short stories published by *Collier's* in the early 1930s.

≈

Remarque's presence in an American mass-circulation magazine like *Collier's* in March 1930—with the story "The Enemy"—was certainly connected to the release of the film of *All Quiet on the Western Front*, which had its New York premiere on April 29, 1930. Remarque was a big enough name after the success of the novel to get a "story by" credit even on the poster for the film, which showed a helmeted soldier looking out of a dark background with wary eyes. He had to be, of course, a German soldier, the protagonist of the film and the novel, Paul Bäumer, played by Lew Ayres in the film—but for an American public he might have been Remarque himself. The *Collier's* story, "The Enemy," concerned German soldiers who secretly fraternized in a friendly way, exchanging cigarettes, with the French enemy on the front. But the face of the "enemy" whom *Collier's* presented to its reading public was the German enemy against whom America had fought, presented by Remarque—as in his novel—in such a way as to engage the sympathy even of those readers who represented Germany's enemies during the past war. The question of who was actually "the enemy" thus became a puzzle of receding perspectives in a figurative hall of historical mirrors—even though that question had seemed to be definitively resolved in the actual Hall of Mirrors with the signing of the Versailles treaty in 1919, ten years before the publication of *All Quiet on the Western Front.*

Though *All Quiet* was published a full decade after the end of the war (it was by no means Remarque's first or overwhelming literary imperative in the 1920s), the novel had its characters living, fighting, and dying in the inescapable present tense that made the war oppressively present to the reader, as well as shockingly real. The stories that began to appear in *Collier's* between 1930 and 1934 did something uncannily different: they looked back on the wartime experience as something remembered across the passage of the decade. "When I asked my school-fellow Lieutenant Ludwig Breyer what was the most vivid experience of all his war service, I expected to hear of Verdun, of the Somme or of Flanders," wrote Remarque in the first sentence of "The Enemy," thus framing a reminiscence that would run counter to expectation, that would refuse to trade in battlefield names that were already famous as history by 1930. Another *Collier's* story from 1930, "Where Karl Had Fought" (even the tense of the title, not present, not even past, but pluperfect) involves revisiting the battlefield: "This is no longer Karl Broeger, the man of the bank managership and the football news; this is another, ten years younger, this is Sergeant Broeger." Never mind that the war is over, it is still very real in the minds of those who survived it. These stories acknowledge the passage of time, ten years out from the peace—and (though no one knew it) ten years from the outbreak of the next war, but they also acknowledge the palpable presence of combat in the routines of ordinary life. Remarque was writing at the midpoint of what we now call the interwar period.

The 1930s was a decade that would be deeply marked by Remarque and his literary depiction of the horrors of war, and ultimately shaped by the failure of such depictions to prevent the next war from coming. The triumph of the film *All Quiet on the Western Front* in 1930—crowned with an Oscar at the end of the year—was supposed to mark the closing of an era with a cinematic tombstone, and not, as we would now see it, the opening sally in a failed campaign to temper the new climate of ominous militarism.

The crucial change that had taken place from 1929 (the novel *All Quiet*) to 1930 (the film *All Quiet*) was, of course, the stock market crash that marked the beginning of the American and the European Depression. In Germany Heinrich Brüning of the Center Party became chancellor in March 1930, just as "The Enemy" appeared in *Collier's*, and Brüning began an unsuccessful effort to combat the Depression through economic austerity measures. Rising unemployment and increased political volatility led to an enormously important election in September 1930, when the hitherto insignificant Nazi Party won more than a hundred seats in the German Reichstag. It was the beginning of the end of the Weimar Republic, the political regime in which Remarque was living and writing as a now famous author. By the end of 1930 the German "enemy" might already have begun to have a different face for some political observers.

The great German cultural event of the spring of 1930, as "The Enemy" was being delivered to homes and newsstands in America, was the production in Berlin of the landmark film by Josef von Sternberg, *The Blue Angel*, starring Emil Jannings as a petty authoritarian schoolteacher destroyed by his infatuation with the cabaret singer Lola Lola—the role that made Marlene Dietrich into an instant legend. The rowdy schoolboys who mock Jannings in *The Blue Angel* form an interesting counterpoint to the docile schoolroom of German boys obediently learning militant patriotism from their teacher in *All Quiet on the Western Front*. Dietrich, who made an anthem out of the song "Falling in Love Again" ("Ich bin von Kopf bis Fuss") would become Remarque's lover later in the decade, and theirs would be an important émigré partnership as a pair of icons who outlived the Weimar culture that created them and successfully reinvented themselves in the United States. By the end of 1930 Dietrich was already in Hollywood with Sternberg, making the film *Morocco*—a film with a rather different message from that of *All Quiet on the Western Front*, as

Sternberg glamorized the military mystique of the French Foreign Legion, with Dietrich slipping off her heels to follow Gary Cooper and his military company into the desert in the final frames.

The Depression in America called for other distractions beyond the historical cinematic tragedy of *All Quiet on the Western Front*, and 1930 was the year that gave the American public Betty Boop and Hostess Twinkies. A *Collier's* cover from March 1930, the month of "The Enemy," showed three fashionable ladies huddled over a silver coffee service, obviously gossiping about anything but World War I, while the cover from August 23, 1930, which included "Where Karl Had Fought," showed a woman in green harem pants, a printed pink and orange kimono-style jacket, and a big multicolored beach ball. The story featured on the cover was not "Where Karl Had Fought" but something called "Sin in the Desert"—which might have fit better with Marlene Dietrich in *Morocco*. *Collier's* did its literary duty by publishing Remarque, but—with its readership of about one and a half million—it also had to offer other entertainments.

In 1934, when the last of these collected Remarque stories appeared in *Collier's*, "On the Road," Remarque was already writing about the Depression in progress, with a story about a man doing railroad labor and remembering a wound from a long-ago war. Between 1930 and 1934, Germany and America had both been radically transformed. Franklin Roosevelt was elected president in Washington and the New Deal had begun. Remarque's sympathy for the war wounded may have mattered less to *Collier's* now than his sympathy for a poor laborer. By 1937 he was already thinking about America when he wrote to Marlene Dietrich in Beverly Hills, "It is night and I am waiting for you to call from New York. The dogs are asleep around me and the gramophone is playing—records that I have found—easy to love—I got you under my skin . . ."[13] The author of *All Quiet on the Western*

Front was responding to the American rhythms of Cole Porter.

≈

In *The Things They Carried*, Tim O'Brien offered a blueprint for the war veteran aspiring to be a writer. A chapter entitled "How to Tell a True War Story" notes, "As a first rule of thumb, you can tell a true war story by its absolute and uncompromising allegiance to obscenity and evil."[14] His observation explains exactly why voices fell silent in the postwar period. Why replay and reanimate the horrors of lived experience? Why fight forgetting? There may, of course, have been many good reasons to forget, but there are even better reasons to remember, as Susan Sontag tells us. "Let the atrocious images haunt us," she writes, "even if they are only tokens, and cannot possibly encompass most of the reality to which they refer, they still perform a vital function. The images say: . . . Don't forget."[15] Remembering serves the collective good, but beyond that, as the field of psychoanalysis discovered, remembering offered a pathway to mental healing and social reintegration for those who had suffered wartime trauma. Psychoanalytic techniques and treatment for processing the past and restoring repressed memories had emerged as powerful tools in the medical arsenal at the turn of the century, but they received an unexpected boost from the collective traumatic experience of World War I combatants and civilians alike.

Some of Remarque's *Collier's* stories can be seen as astonishingly close to Freud's case studies. They may take the form of fiction, but they are based on fact, often more solidly credible than what we find in, say, Freud and Breuer's *Studies in Hysteria*, written by two male doctors analyzing female "hysterics." Remarque gives us presenting symptoms, manifestations of a pathology, and a pathway to a cure via remembering, reenacting, and abreacting in moments of therapeutic release.

Remarque's snapshots of war neuroses and their consequences and cures remind us that World War I vastly expanded the domain of those treatable with psychoanalysis. The British anthropologist, neurologist, and psychiatrist W. H. R. Rivers (fictionally memorialized in Pat Barker's *Regeneration*) had once decided to "go in for insanity" after trying out a number of career options. But during the war he discovered that the "insane" now included victims of shell shock, men whose symptoms included temporary blindness, memory loss, paralysis— what could, in short, by analogy with the patients of Freud and Breuer, be called male hysteria. The British had tried hard to avoid the feminizing term "hysteria," even though combat afflictions resembled that disorder, choosing instead "shell shock," which suggests physical rather than mental trauma and was, for that reason, favored over "anxiety neurosis," "war strain," and "soldier's heart."[16] Astonishingly, Freud had presciently developed a cure even before the mass onset of the disorder. "Just as

Freud's theory of the unconscious and the method of psycho-analysis founded upon it should be so hotly discussed," Rivers noted, "there should have occurred events which have produced on an enormous scale just those considerations of paralysis and contracture, phobia and obsession, which the theory was designed to explain."

What Rivers learned while treating, among others, Siegfried Sassoon and Wilfred Owen, was that Freud's discovery of repression, his belief in the process of "active suppression of unpleasant experience" and how it leads to repetition compulsion, offered the key to recovery from shell shock. Rivers practiced at Craiglockhart, a hospital for officers, where soldiers were not subjected to the painful electric faradization or electric shock therapy and instead engaged in a talking cure with a physician trained in psychiatric practices.

If we look at the *Collier's* story "Josef's Wife," we begin to see just how closely Remarque modeled his short stories on case studies, drawing us first into the orbit of his protagonist's daily life, then opening a window into his mental world. That story gives readers an account of Corporal Josef Thiedemann, a man buried alive by a trench mortar in 1918 and back home the following year, retrieved by his devoted wife. A victim of amnesia, he reenacts the wartime trauma at home: "He often suffered at night from attacks of suffocation. Then he would leap up and strike out about him and scream." Occasionally he becomes "restless" and flings himself on the ground: "He wanted to crawl and kept ducking continually." Josef's wife, featured in the title, is stoically persistent and instinctively understands how to treat her husband.

What does Josef's wife do, given the fact that her husband is unable to escape his condition with the talking cure that W. H. R. Rivers adapted from Freud and Breuer's *Studies on Hysteria*? Rivers had written about the "natural tendency to banish the distressing or horrible," along with "all thoughts of war" and how it could be damaging rather than healing. He noted that many physicians advocated focusing on "beautiful scenery" or "other pleasant aspects of experience" when in fact the "cessation of repression" can relieve some of the distressing aftershocks of traumatic experience. Beyond providing support, warmth, and purposefully affectless care, Josef's wife takes her husband back to the scene of the traumatic event with the hope of enabling him to confront, remember, and abreact, with unexpected support from scavengers searching for scrap metal on the battlefields. In the setting of a double cleanup operation, Remarque brilliantly captures the ravages of war, taking us inside a mind that has been shattered and outdoors into a landscape utterly devastated by explosive weapons.

Reenactment occasionally gives way to forms of repetition compulsion that are depleting and damaging rather than cathartic and healing, as is the case for Karl Broeger in "Where Karl Had Fought," a witness narrative with a comrade who reports Karl's struggle with war trauma. Karl lives in a spatio-temporal zone that blurs the lines between past and present, war and peace, civilian life and combat. As he and the narrator embark on a "sight-seeing tour" of theaters of war, the "deathways of yesterday" are transformed into "boulevards of respectable post-factum visitors." When remembrance bursts in on Karl "like a whirlwind," he becomes the "dodging, intent, cautious gliding" beast of the battlefields: "once again he leads his men through the shell holes to the assault on the town." We are caught in a Kafkaesque eternal present, a prison house of the mind where trauma is ceaselessly repeated. As the two pass through a landscape devoted to memorialization, complete with tour guides, monuments, and fourteen thousand crosses, Karl experiences surges of what Toni Morrison called rememory, a process of invoking memory images that are both in the mind and out in the world. Armed with this kind of double vision and double consciousness—what could be seen as layered recollections—Karl revisits a scene of battle and reenacts terror, loss, and mourning, struggling to let go of his memories to use what Rivers termed *autognosis*, the ability to achieve some kind of healing by working through war memories.

≈

If the "case studies" published by *Collier's* model the successes and failures of psychotherapeutic strategies for working through war trauma, the other stories published there in the 1930s offer compelling dramatizations of the consequences of combat. Set in Germany during the war and in its aftermath, they take the form of what Margot Norris has called the literary vignette, a genre that "reduces the scale and magnitude of modern war violence sufficiently to retrieve an imaginable community of victims available to empathy and identification."[17] These moving miniatures are also testimonials, charged descriptions of traumatic experience that reach out and grab us, drawing us into a universe of intense suffering with their haunting accounts.[18] If compassion and empathy can quickly succumb to defeat for combatants facing violence that spirals out of control ("We have become wild beasts," Paul Bäumer tells us in *All Quiet on the Western Front*), they remain powerful forces for those outside the combat zone, reminders of a "spark of humanity in the midst of annihilation," as we read in "Annette's Love Story."

By writing stories designed to elicit empathy, thereby promoting what separates humans from beasts, Remarque performed what he must have seen as cultural work beyond pacifism. As Elaine Scarry has pointed out, "the fact of injuring tends to be absent from strategic and political descriptions of war," which tend to mask the fact that "the central goal of war is to out-injure the opponent."[19] In *Good-bye to All That*, published like *All Quiet on the Western Front* in 1929, Robert Graves describes this disjunction and how it was effaced in the final months of the war:

> *Infantry Training*, 1914, laid it down politely that the soldier's ultimate aim was to put out of action or render ineffective the armed forces of the enemy. The War Office no longer considered this statement direct enough for war attrition. Troops learned instead that they must HATE the Germans, and KILL as many of them as possible.... "Hurt him, now! In at the belly! Tear his guts out!" they would scream.... "BITE HIM, I SAY! STICK YOUR TEETH IN HIM AND WORRY HIM! EAT HIS HEART OUT!"[20]

As a counterbalance to the abstractions of numbers of wounded and body counts, as well as to disquisitions on military valor and honor, Remarque used his verbal resources to put injury on display, not to incite to violence but to show the explosive effects of war machinery and weapons on the fragile human body. In the *Collier's* stories, a voice emerges, one able to say what veterans could not say, recruiting our sense of empathy, building bridges between the living and the wounded or dead, and creating small patches of light and warmth in the darkness.

In the story ironically entitled "The Enemy," Remarque reveals the one steadying force in a soldier's life and how comradeship sustained the men, even as it, inevitably, magnified suffering when tragedy struck. In an episode that resonates with the famous Christmas truce of 1914, when German, French, and British soldiers crossed battle lines to fraternize, the narrator reports that the war's "most vivid experience" turns out to be, not Verdun, the Somme, or Flanders, but the tragic death of a Frenchman accidently caught in the line of fire during a cease-fire. Weapons have a transformative power, and it is the dark "magic" of weapons that turns men against each other, escalating hostilities and turning comrades into enemies. As in *All Quiet*

on the Western Front and in later novels, comradeship (*Kameradschaft*) became a sustaining force,
and a reminder that national identity has a way of
deforming human interactions, leading to antago-
nism where there are in fact no fundamental differ-
ences between the men on the two sides.[21] But that
camaraderie perversely backfires, for the weapons
of the war quickly can work their magic in a single,
random instant of betrayal. As one critic puts it,
compassion becomes "an instrument of torture to
those afflicted by it."[22]

For Remarque, writing is a response to loss,
an attempt not just to recapture sensation but to
mine some kind of redemptive meaning from the
carnage and the ruins. "Silence," the most melancholy of the stories in this volume, draws its wistful
power from the recognition that war destroys not
only worlds but also words, undoing language and
its power to memorialize. "Above this pall broods
the silence, and sorrow and memory," Remarque
writes, reminding readers that "beside the dead sol-

diers sleep their weapons" (the unexploded shells still on the battlefield). Scavengers searching for scrap metal on the battlefields engage in a kind of violation, one that is not without risk. Remarque's meditation on the brooding silence of the battle-fields suggests that attempts to remember and me-morialize may be just as intrusive and perilous as the exploitative labors of the scavengers.

If "Silence" mutes voices and advocates hushed reverence for the dead, "I Dreamt Last Night" of-fers a hymn to the bonding power of music and uses the power of narrative to memorialize a dead man. Witnessing an act of compassion, the hospitalized narrator finds his way back to life through the dis-covery of "something else," something above and beyond "war and destruction." In an interesting twist, *Collier's* billed the story as follows: "The au-thor of 'All Quiet on the Western Front' interrupts his long silence to write this grave and magnificent story." The first-person account about Gerhart Brockman, an army officer who has been "dying uninterruptedly for weeks," ends as a testimony to the power of language. Though unable to halt death, the sorcery of words at least provides some kind of consolation, if only in its power to move us as we read about how others are moved by loss. The stark prose of the *Collier's* English-language translations seems also to create a literary masculine association between Remarque and his American contemporary Hemingway, who was likewise committed to exploring the fictional dimensions of war.

Empathetic identification is the delivered effect in many of Remarque's vignettes, but these redemptive moments are tempered by other stories in which "moving" comes to mean nothing more than a nomadic existence on the fringes of the social world. In "The Strange Fate of Johann Bartok," the protagonist tenaciously holds on to the memory of his wife through the war years only to return home and discover that his wife's memory is not as durable. Like the first-person narrator of "On the Road," who experiences acts of kindness and generosity in ways that are unnerving rather than empowering, Bartok moves on, searching for a way back through the distractions of work. Bartok, with his Hungarian surname, comes out of the Habsburg wartime world that we more usually associate with the fiction of Joseph Roth, who was also remembering the war in the early 1930s, most famously as the terrible culmination of the novel *Radetzky March*, which was published in 1932.

≈

Remarque revisits the war in large part to carry some of its victims out of the combat zone and the precincts of silence into the public domain. The German war correspondent Carolin Emcke once explained why she traveled to war zones. "The experience of violence," she wrote, "often leads to the inability to give an account of the injustice endured, to the speechlessness of the victim, to their being forgotten."[23] Remarque wrote the stories that the combatants themselves could not tell, not only because some became casualties of war but also because of the language-shattering experience of violence. Violence "has no voice," Elaine Scarry tells us, for it "resists language and destroys it, . . . reverts to the state anterior to language."[24]

That German readers identified with Paul Bäumer is not in the least surprising. But as we can surmise from the sale of nearly nine million copies in the United States over nine decades— never mind that the novel was also translated into sixty languages—Remarque's novel has also built a substantial community of readers who effortlessly cross national lines to empathize with its protagonist. Mordecai Richler, to his own shocked amazement, read the book in 1944 and found that "the author had seduced me into identifying with my enemy, 19-year-old Paul Bäumer, thrust into the bloody trenches of World War I."[25]

Why this American solidarity with a German soldier fighting the Allied Powers? Why do we fraternize in such powerful ways with a man who was once an enemy combatant? There is, after all, a clear difference between bonding with the war dead on your own side and identifying with the suffering of enemy combatants. For one thing, the German soldiers in Remarque's novels and stories quickly learn that the enemy is not, say, the Frenchman with his sights trained across no-man's-land, but generals, factory owners, even schoolteachers, and other opportunistic players from what, only following World War II, a U.S. president called the military-industrial complex. Combatants on both sides are in its iron grip, and the German *Muschkoten*, like British tommies, U.S. doughboys, and French *poilus*, are all victims. The more we are exposed to the interior lives of Remarque's soldiers and veterans, the more we are drawn into the orbit of their sufferings in ways that might lead us to put a novel like *All Quiet on the Western Front* down, close it up, and decide, as Bob Dylan tells us he did in his 2017 Nobel acceptance speech, "I never wanted to read another war novel again, and I never did."[26] But as the *Collier's* stories reveal, there is far more to Remarque than what is told in that one novel, and the accounts of those who survived and suffered, struggled and strategized, reminisced and convalesced, deserve as much attention as the tributes to those who tragically never returned from the combat zone.

NOTES

1 Alden Whitman, "Erich Maria Remarque Is Dead," *New York Times*, 26 September 1970.

2 Ibid.

3 Hilton Tims, *Erich Maria Remarque: The Last Romantic* (New York: Carroll & Graf, 2003), 119.

4 Christine R. Barker and R. W. Last, *Erich Maria Remarque* (London: Oswald Wolff, 1979), 24.

5 Tims, *Erich Maria Remarque*, 119.

6 Ibid., 120.

7 Barker and Last, *Erich Maria Remarque*, 7.

8 Walter Benjamin, "The Storyteller: Reflections on the Works of Nikolai Leskov," in *Illuminations: Essays and Reflections*, ed. Hannah Arendt (New York: Schocken, 1969), 59–68.

9 Simon Schama, *The Power of Art* (New York: HarperCollins, 2006), 363.

10 Franz Marc, *Letters from the War*, ed. Klaus Lankheit and Uwe Steffen, trans. Liselotte Dieckmann (New York: Peter Lang, 1992), 34.

11 Sarah Cole, "People in War," in *The Cambridge Companion to War Writing*, ed. Kate McLoughlin (Cambridge: Cambridge University Press, 2009), 25–37, 35.

12 "See New War Spirit in German Film Row," *New York Times*, 7 December 1930.

13 *"Sag mir, dass Du mich liebst. . . .": Erich Maria Remarque—Marlene Dietrich, Zeugnisse einer Leidenschaft*, ed. Werner Fuld and Thomas Schneider (Cologne: Kiepenheuer & Witsch, 2001), 25 November 1937, 23.

14 Tim O'Brien, *The Things They Carried* (New York: Mariner, 2009), 66.

15 Susan Sontag, *Regarding the Pain of Others* (New York: Farrar, Straus & Giroux, 2003), 115.

16 Elaine Showalter, "Hysteria, Feminism, and Gender," in *Hysteria beyond Freud*, ed. Sander L. Gilman et al. (Berkeley: University of California Press, 1993), 286–334, 321.

17 Margot Norris, *Writing War in the Twentieth Century* (Charlottesville: University of Virginia Press, 2000), 28.

18 The evocative value of testimony has been more fully explored in the context of the Holocaust by Dori Laub and Shoshana

Felman in *Testimony: Crises of Witnessing in Literature, Psychoanalysis and History* (New York: Routledge, 1992).

19 Elaine Scarry, *The Body in Pain: The Making and Unmaking of the World* (New York: Oxford University Press, 1985), 12.

20 Robert Graves, *Good-bye to All That* (New York: Random House, Vintage, 1998), 237.

21 Wilhelm J. Schwarz, *War and the Mind of Germany* (Bern: Herbert Lang; Frankfurt a.M.: Peter Lang, 1975), 25.

22 Norris, *Writing War*, 94.

23 Carolin Emcke, *Echoes of Violence: Letters from a War Reporter* (Princeton: Princeton University Press, 2007), 199.

24 Scarry, *The Body in Pain*, 17.

25 Mordecai Richler, "1944: The Year I Learned to Love a German," *New York Times*, 2 February 1986.

26 Bob Dylan, "Nobel Lecture," 5 June 2017, www.nobelprize.org.

Eight Stories

1

THE ENEMY

When I asked my school-fellow Lieutenant Ludwig Breyer what was the most vivid experience of all his war service, I expected to hear of Verdun, of the Somme or of Flanders; for he had been on all three fronts during the worst months. But instead of that he told me the following:

Not the most vivid, but the most enduring of my impressions began as we lay resting in a little French village far behind the lines. We had been in a nasty place, where the shelling had been extremely severe, and had come farther back than usual, because we had suffered heavily and needed to be brought up to strength again.

It was a glorious week in August, a marvelous St. Luke's summer, and it went to our heads like the rich, golden wine we once found in a cellar in Champagne. We had been deloused; a few of us had even come by clean linen; the others were boiling their shirts thoroughly at small fires; everywhere was an atmosphere of cleanliness—the magic of which only a mud-caked soldier knows—friendly as a Saturday evening in the far-off days of peace, when, as children, we were bathed in the big tub and Mother brought out the fresh linen, smelling of starch, Sunday and cake, from the cupboard.

You know, of course, it is no fairy tale when I say that the sense of this declining August afternoon moved, sweet and strong, in my veins. A soldier has a far different relationship with nature from that of most men. All the thousand inhibitions, the barriers and constraints fall away before the hard, the terrible existence on the borders of death; and during the minutes and the hours of respite, in the days out resting, the idea of *life*, the mere fact of being still there, of having come through, would sometimes swell into sheer joy at being able to see, and to breathe and to move freely about.

A field under the evening sun, the blue shadows of a wood, the rustle of a poplar, the clear flood of running waters, were then a joy beyond naming; but deep down in it, like a whip, like a thorn, lay the sharp pain of the knowledge that in a few hours, in a few days, all this must be left behind, changed once more for the seared landscapes of death. And this feeling, so strangely compounded out of happiness, pain, melancholy, grief, desire and hopelessness, was the common experience of a soldier out resting.

After supper I walked with some comrades a short distance beyond the village. We did not talk much; for the first time in weeks we were perfectly content, and warmed ourselves in the slanting rays of the sun as it shone full into our faces. Thus we came at length on a small, stark factory standing in the middle of a large enclosure, around which sentries were posted. The yard was full of prisoners, awaiting transport into Germany.

Without ceremony the sentries allowed us in and we were able to look about us. Several hundreds of Frenchmen were assembled there. They sat or lay about, smoked, talked and dozed. It was an eye-opener to me. Until that time I had had only rapid, fleeting glimpses—single, phantom-like—of the men that held the opposing trenches. A helmet, perhaps, rising for a moment above the level of the parapet; an arm, that flung and disappeared again; a patch of gray-blue cloth, a figure springing up into the air—almost abstract things they were, lurking behind fire of rifles, behind hand grenades and wire entanglements.

Here for the first time I saw prisoners, lots of them, sitting, lying, smoking—Frenchmen without weapons.

I felt a sudden shock; then a moment later I had to laugh at myself. It had shocked me that they should be just men like ourselves. But the fact was—strange enough, God knows—I had simply never thought about it before. Frenchmen? They were enemies who were to be killed, because they wanted to destroy Germany. But in that August evening I learned the baleful secret, the magic of weapons. Weapons transfigure men. And these harmless fellows, these factory hands, laborers, tradesmen, schoolboys, now sitting around so quiet and resigned, had they but weapons, on the instant would turn once again into enemies.

THE BATTLE OF MATERIALS

Originally they were no enemies; not until they got weapons did they become so. It made me ponder, though I knew well enough that my logic was perhaps not perfectly sound. But the idea dawned on me that it was weapons that had forced the war on us. There were so many weapons in the world that in the end they got the upper hand over men and turned them into enemies. . . .

And then much later, up in Flanders, I perceived the same thing once more: while the battle of materials raged on, there was practically no use whatever for men any more. The materials just hurled themselves against one another in mad fury. A man could not help feeling that when everything that lay between the weapons was dead, the weapons themselves would go on of their own accord to the utter annihilation of the world.

But here in the factory yard I saw only men like ourselves. And for the first time I understood that it was against men I was fighting; men, bewitched like ourselves by strong words and weapons; men, who had wives, children, parents and callings, and who, perhaps—if the suggestion had come to me from them—must even now be awakening also and looking about them in just the same way and asking: "Brothers, what is it we are doing here? What is all this?"

Some few weeks later we were back on a very quiet sector. The French line came up fairly close

to our own, but both the positions were well fortified and, as I say, there was almost nothing doing
at all. Punctually at seven each morning the artillery would exchange a few shots by way of greeting;
then at noon would come another little salute, and
at nightfall the usual benediction. We used to take
sun-baths in front of our dugouts and would risk
taking off our boots at night to sleep.

One day, on the other side of No Man's Land,
there appeared suddenly over the parapet a placard with this inscription: "*Attention!*" As you may
imagine, we just stared at it in astonishment. Then
at last we decided they just wanted to warn us there
was to be an extra artillery strafe, over and above
the usual program; so we held ourselves in readiness to disappear down into the dugouts at the
sound of the first shot.

But all remained quiet. The placard vanished.
Then a few seconds later up came a spade, and resting on the blade we could make out a large box of
cigarettes. One of our fellows who had some idea

of the language, painted the word "*Compris*" on the back of a cardboard box in boot polish. We hoisted up the box. Then on the other side they waved the box of cigarettes to and fro. And we waved our box in response. Then up came a piece of white cloth.

In all haste we seized Lance Corporal Bühler's shirt from off his knees as he sat delousing himself, and waved it.

A PRIVATE PEACE

After a time the white cloth on the other side rose up and a helmet appeared. We waved our shirt harder, till the lice must have rained out of it. An arm was thrust up, holding a packet. And then a man clambered slowly out through the barbed wire; on hands and knees he crawled towards us from time to time waving a handkerchief and laughing excitedly. About the middle of No Man's Land he came to a halt and put down his packet.

He pointed to it several times, laughed, beckoned and crawled back.

We were in a rare state of excitement. Mingled with the almost boyish feeling of doing something that was forbidden, the feeling of snapping our fingers at somebody, and the mere crude desire to get possession of the good things set there in front of us, was a breath of freedom, of independence, of triumph over all the mechanism of death. I had the same feeling as when I stood there among the prisoners, as though something human had burst victoriously through the bare concept of "the enemy," and I wanted to contribute my share to the triumph.

Hastily we collected a few gifts, sorry things they were indeed, for we had far less to give than the fellows over yonder. Then we renewed our signals with the shirt and were duly answered. Slowly I heaved myself up; my head and shoulders stood clear. It was a damned awful minute, that I can tell you, standing there unprotected, clear above the parapet.

Then I crawled right out; and now my thoughts changed completely as though they had suddenly been thrown over into reverse gear. The strange situation took hold on me; I felt a strong, exuberant gayety rise up in me; happy and laughing I scampered swiftly across on all fours. And I was aware of one prodigious minute of peace—a solitary, a private peace, peace through the whole world for my sake.

I set down my things, picked up the others and crept back. And in that moment the peace collapsed. I was conscious again of a hundred rifle barrels pointed at my back. A terrible fear laid hold on me and the sweat poured out of me like water from a spring. But I regained the trench unharmed and lay down panting.

FRIENDLY MEETINGS

By next day I was quite used to the business; and subsequently we simplified it, so that we no longer went out one after the other, but both of us climbed out of our trenches at the same moment. Like two dogs left off the chain, we crept over to each other and exchanged our gifts.

The first time that we came face to face we just smiled at each other in embarrassment. The other fellow was a young chap like myself, twenty years of age perhaps. You could see in his face how good a joke he thought it. "*Bonjour, camarade,*" said he; but I was so taken aback that I said, "*Bonjour, bonjour,*" repeating it, twice, three times, and nodded and hastily turned back.

We had a definite time for meeting, and the preliminary signaling was dropped, because both sides observed the unwritten peace treaty. And an hour later we were blazing away at one another again as before. Once, with a slight hesitation, the other fellow stretched out his hand to me and we shook hands. It was queer.

At that time similar incidents were taking place on other parts of the front also. The High Command got wind of it, and orders had already been issued to the effect that such things were absolutely forbidden; on some occasions it had even interfered with the daily round of hostilities. But that did not bother us.

One day a major turned up in the line and gave us a personal lecture. He was very officious and energetic and told us that he meant to stay up in the line until nightfall. Unluckily he took up his post close by our sally point, and demanded a rifle. He was a very young major, itching for action.

We did not know what we should do. There was no possibility of giving the fellows over there a signal; and besides, we thought we might get shot there and then on the spot for having dealings with the enemy. The minute hand of my watch advanced slowly. Nothing happened, and it almost looked as though things might go off smoothly.

No doubt the major only knew of the general fraternization that had been going on along the front, but nothing definite as to what we had been up to here; it was nothing but sheer bad luck that brought him here just now and gave him that job to do.

I meditated whether I should say to him, "In five minutes there will be someone coming from over there. We must not shoot; he trusts us." But I did not dare; and anyway what would have been the use? If I did he might, perhaps just stay on and wait, whereas now there was always a chance he would go. Besides, Bühler whispered to me how he had crept behind one of the breastworks and waved a "wash-out" with his rifle (the way one signals a miss on a rifle range), and they had waved back. They had understood they must not come.

Fortunately the day was dull; it was raining a little and darkness was coming on. Already it was a quarter of an hour past the time fixed for our meeting. We were beginning to breathe again. Then suddenly my eyes stared; my tongue lay like a lump in my mouth; I wanted to cry out and could not; rigid and horrified I stared across No Man's Land and saw an arm slowly show itself, then a body. Bühler dashed around the breastwork and tried desperately to signal a warning. But it was too late. The major had already fired. With a thin cry the body sank back again.

TO DROWN THE CRY

For a moment there was a weird stillness. Then we heard a bellow and a withering fire set in. "Shoot! They are coming," yelled the major.

Then we opened fire also. We loaded and fired like madmen, loaded and fired simply to put that awful moment behind us. The entire front was roused, the guns even joined in, and it went on the whole night. By morning we had lost twelve men, the major and Bühler amongst them.

From that time on the hostilities were satisfactorily maintained; cigarettes changed hands no more;

and the casualty figures were larger. Many things happened to me after that. I saw many a man die; I myself killed more than one; I became hard and insensible. The years went by. But in all the long time I have not dared think on that thin cry in the rain.

2

SILENCE

No man can say exactly when it begins: but suddenly the smooth, gently rounded lines of the horizon alter; the red and brown, the bright burning colors of the leaves of the forest take on all at once a queer tone, the fields fade and wither to ocher tints; something strange, still, pallid is in the landscape, and one is at a loss to explain it.

It is the same range of hills, the same woods, the same fields and meadows as before, still the same countryside as an hour ago; there runs the road, white and endless far out across it, and the golden light of late autumn is still poured out on the earth like sweet wine—and yet, invisible, inaudible, something has come into it out of the distance; vast, solemn and powerful, suddenly it stands there, and overshadows all.

It is not those crosses that show up every moment, thin and dark at the roadside. Lopsided and very tired they stick up there in the turf, wasted by many winds, weary of flying clouds, the crosses of the war of 1870. Slender saplings planted beside them in those days have long since grown into trees with great branches full of twittering birds. These old trenches are no longer hideous, there is scarcely the suggestion of death about them now—already they are like parkland, picturesque and lovely, good earth and country.

It is not the character of this fair, fearful region, that has always been a battle-ground and where for centuries war has cast its deposit, like the separate strata in a rock, deposit on deposit, layer upon layer, war upon war, discernible even today, from the struggles of the French kings up to the trenches of Mars la Tour and the serried cemeteries of Douaumont.

Nor is it the mysterious twofold spirit of this ground, where the soft, blue lines on the horizon are not hills and woodlands simply, but concealed forts; the smooth summits in front of them not just chains of hills, but strong, fortified heights; idyllic valleys serving also as entrenchments, death's valleys, rendezvous, battle approaches; and the little hillocks are concrete gun-emplacements, nests of machine guns, honeycombed with magazines and tunnels; for here everything has been turned into strategy. Strategy and tombs.

It is the silence. The dreadful silence of Verdun. The silence after the battle. A silence without parallel in the world; for in all contests hitherto nature, at the last, has regained the upper hand; life just grew up again out of the destruction, towns were rebuilt, woods flourished once more and within a few months new corn waved in the fields. But in this last, most terrible of wars destruction has for the first time gained victory. Here stood villages that have never been rebuilt; villages of which not a stone now stands. The ground beneath them is still so full of threatening death, full of live explosives, of shells, mines and poisonous gasses, that every stroke of the mattock, every thrust of the spade is dangerous. Here were trees that have never grown again, because not only their tops and trunks, but their roots also were ripped away, shattered and smashed into splinters. Fields were here where the plow will never go again because their sowing has been of steel, steel and more steel.

In the shell-holes of this pitted land, there does grow, it is true, a wild, disheveled, wan grass. Round their edges, too, flower red poppies and camomile, and even a shrub sometimes creeps up, frowsy and timid, out of the level of the waste; but this scant growth merely strengthens the impression of the silence and desolation. It is as though there were at this place a hole in the running rib-

bon of events, as though Time stood still here;
Time, that carries in itself not things past only, but
also things to come, as though here in its compassion, it shuts off its engine. There is no land like this
elsewhere in the world; a desert is more living, for
its stillness is organic.

There is no silence like this one in the world, for
this silence is a stupendous, petrified cry. There is
nothing in it of the quiet of the graveyard; for there
among the many weary, spent lives sleeps little that
was ardent and young; but here for hundreds of
thousands that great power standing in their eyes,
the force that let them breathe, and see, and duck,
and fight, was suddenly shivered to atoms: here
in the convulsion of tensest self-defense Life was
coveted, cherished, believed in, more passionately,
more wildly, more fervently, more madly than ever;
and in upon this distraught, straining will, this boiling whirlpool of activity, torment, hope, fear, greed
of life, burst the hail of splinters and bullets. Then
the toughest, frailest thing there is, Life, poured

out its blood, and the great darkness came down upon eight hundred thousand men.

Above these fields the lost years seem to stand, the years that have not been fulfilled—the call of the unlived life, that finds no rest—the cry of youth quenched too soon, in full career come to its end. Surely at night they burst up from the earth like ghostly blue fire.

Down from the heights comes a gray, leaden wind and mingles with the autumn glow, its bright fire and golden light. Down from the heights comes the stillness that makes a cheerful day peaked and spiritless, as though the sun had been darkened as in that afternoon on Golgotha. Down from the heights come names and memories. Vaux, Thiaumont, Belleville, Cold Earth, Death Valley, Hill 304, Dead Man—what names! Four long years they lived beneath the gigantic clamor of death; today they grip you fast in the endlessness of their silence. No Cook's parties, no convenient one-day excursions at reasonable prices, with visits to deep dugouts by romantic carbide-light, can alter it. This land belongs to the dead.

But in this earth that has been churned over and over by shells of every caliber, in this land of stiffened horror, this place of craters, there live men. One hardly sees them, so well have they adapted themselves as time has passed, so little do they stand out from their surroundings. Their clothes are yellow and gray and dirty with their toil. Sometimes they are in hundreds, sometimes they must number thousands, but they work singly and are so scattered that they always seem to be but few— industrious little ants in the hollow craters. They live a life to themselves, often they stay for months together in their black hutments and rarely come into the villages. They are the seekers.

The battlefields have become propositions for speculative exploitation. A contractor has obtained a permit from the government to salvage all the valuable metal. He employs the seekers to do it. They hunt for everything with metal value, old rifles, dud shells, bombs, railway lines, rolls of wire, spades—these fields of memory, of stillness and sorrow are iron, steel and copper mines to them. They like copper most. It brings the best price.

Almost all the seekers are Russians. In the silence, they too have become silent. They mostly keep to themselves. No men desire their company; though the government grant a thousand permits, still one feels it is not right what they do. There are millions of francs' worth of metal in that earth; there are also tears, blood and anguish of millions.

It is a profitable business, and many of the seekers can soon buy themselves motor cars. For years together the artillery saw to it that they should not lack sustenance. The first, hasty, superficial gleaning is over, and now they must dig down to the next layer of buried treasure. The soil is tough, and they have been working a week already on one pit a couple of yards square. Therefore it is imperative to discover likely places. That requires experience.

Usually the ground is first sounded for metal by means of long spikes which are driven down into the earth. Now it may happen that one lands on a boot that offers resistance; for the boots of the dead down below there are commonly still well-preserved; but a seeker can tell that; he has had practice. He can generally tell from above ground whether the excavation will be worth his while or not. If he strikes a steel helmet, well and good; that has its value as locating a possible prize.

There are some old, experienced searchers who only dig in places where a shrub of some kind has sprung up. They consider that in such places there must be buried dugouts with corpses in them—otherwise the bush would not have grown so well. And in dugouts there are usually all sorts of metal to be had.

If a man is in luck, he may hit a machine gun, or even a small dump. Then, of course, some thousands of francs are made at one scoop. One find of which they still talk was an excavated German plane. In the pilot's seat the skeleton was still squatting, and between his legs lay a box with 15,000 gold marks.

It is everywhere the same picture. The earth is first loosened and dug up, and then further turned over with the hands. Bombs, German ones with long handles, and a dixie, come to light. They arouse little interest. A rifle-barrel, on the other hand, bent and corroded, is put with the heap of rusted iron which has been collected already. A helmet—then a pallid, damp rag, gray-green, threadbare, already half turned to clay, a skull, with hair still on it, fair hair, a skull with a splintered hole smashed in the forehead. The seeker puts it in a little box behind him. From the miserable, dirty-green rag he shakes out spotted brown bones. The last ones he hauls out of the boot tops. All goes into the box, to be sent at evening to the central depot for identification. A rotted purse with a little blackened money stays lying there. The remnant of a pocketbook, quite rotten, also. But now the spade rings on metal once again, iron stakes and rolls of wire appear—good find—

It is always the same picture, a hundred times, a thousand times; in the autumn sunshine lies a soldier, a few rotten rags, a few bones, a skull, a bit of equipment with a rust-clotted buckle, a cartridge pouch. He too would be glad enough to be living this hour.

Some seekers reckon to be able to tell by the shape of the jawbone whether they are looking at a German skull or a French one. And it is important that the bones should be brought back to the central depot in the evening, otherwise the foxes would eat them by morning. It is queer, that— here foxes eat bones. There is certainly nothing else for them to eat. And yet there are lots of foxes here.

The seekers squat in their countless little pot-holes and dig like moles. True, the bones that they do find are identified, assembled in cemeteries, in mausoleums, in huge stone coffins. Yet perhaps it were better to let these soldiers rest where they have rested now for ten or twelve years, comrades all.

And it is as though they themselves would not have it otherwise. It is as though the earth itself kept watch over them and defended them against the hands that grope among them after metal and money. For beside the dead soldiers sleep their weapons. And often their weapons still retain the power to strike.

A blow with a mattock on the ground is enough. A sharp spade-thrust will suffice, and the ground bursts up with a dull roar, splinters fly, and death with swift hand reaches out of the earth to the seeker. Already many have been torn to pieces, many mutilated, and every week fresh ones join them. Death, that first cut down the soldiers, now watches over the graves of the slain, and the earth keeps them as though they ought not to lie in magnificent mausoleums but remain where they have fallen.

And above this pall Time has come to a stand, before the anguish ringed within these horizons; above this pall broods the silence, and sorrow and memory.

3

WHERE KARL HAD FOUGHT

The car sweeps over the road with the throttle full open, the tires sing, the road is straight, the windows rattle softly and Strasbourg and Metz are already far behind us. Beside me sits Karl Broeger, eating a buttered roll, but not with full concentration. His thoughts are elsewhere.

It is two hours since we lunched. After we recover from the pleasant surprise of a half lobster-mayonnaise at twenty-five francs as *hors d'oeuvre*, not to mention a competence of other things appetizing, and the immense platter of cheese at that memorable meal, Karl begins to give me a full account of his plans and chances for the future.

I do not understand a great deal of it, for there is a heap of ifs and buts, and of calculations and persons in it. Whether it is the result of the lobster, or the wine, or perhaps even the amazing cheapness of them both, his prospects pile one on another till they lose themselves in the clouds of Mount Everest—in ten years he will be manager, in twenty, director, general-director, president and so on. At present Karl stands on a rung of the ladder sufficiently low to insure that he shall be able to fall off without seriously hurting himself. He is a bank clerk and has a sound constitution. For that reason, two hours after the lobster, he is already eating again—a good, plain, buttered roll. Meanwhile, not to be beforehand with the realization of his ideals, he occupies himself dreaming of what he will do when once he becomes manager. That is Karl.

The car races on through the villages—steep gables, cows, women's colored dresses, autumn breeze and dungheaps spin past our windows, curve after curve, rise after rise, till the avenues and trees cease; the roads fork and become narrower; heavy, lumbering busses with fat letters and devices painted on them approach us, and on the signboards names appear at which all must stand still.

Karl packs up his pocket-book. Stuffed in with technical bank papers, he has clippings from a sporting paper describing the glorious football match, Rheine vs. Münster (Karl's team won in a walk-over, 6–0, and Karl was picked out for special praise), but the weightiest items are some portraits of debonair ladies, which he had been contemplating by way of dessert.

Ahead of us the road comes to an end. The car halts with a grinding of brakes; we climb out and stand in a kind of market place. Motors are parking, anxious chauffeurs stand about, all efficiency in their high-peaked motor-caps, flocks of people assemble and get into formations, guides hunt about, gathering their lambs, and march off.

All around us in subdued, hasty whispers men ply their business assiduously; the death-ways of yesterday are changed now to boulevards of respectable post-factum visitors, and yonder, where once every step meant blood, and choking, terrible fear in the throat, today run wood-paved ways to keep the tourists' shoes clean, and well-schooled interpreters march before, so that everyone shall see everything—everything guaranteed. Douaumont.

About us, too, someone buzzes, excited, ready and eager—he will explain to us the strategy of the affairs here, put us *au fait* with the more recondite aspects of the matter, so to speak. Karl, fortified with his lobster and buttered roll, smiling graciously, gives ear, and we also allow ourselves to be shown over the fort by carbide light; we, too, have it explained to us how practical the Germans were, in that no sooner had they taken over the fort than they installed machinery in the basements, installed electric lights and constructed cranes to hoist up the munitions, none of which had been there before.

Karl nods affirmation: Yes, that was so. But as we stand before the rusty steel helmets, the twisted rifle barrels and dud shells, and the guide starts prating here also, and a second opens up beside us with the same tale in English, Karl beckons; he has had enough; we push our way out into the open. He has grown silent before the helmets, the breastplates, the splinters of shell down below there.

Outside, after the stifling air of the tunnel, a breeze comes to meet us, so soft and gentle one would like to lean against it. It is still quite light, but it is already that mysterious hour when the day and the night hang equal on the beam, the pans of the balance in their ceaseless oscillation pause for a moment and seem to stand still—a heartbeat more and the magic is gone, a faint glimmer of evening is suddenly there, a cow bellows in the meadow and night has begun.

Wave upon wave the heights lie before us in violent shadow. The guide has followed us and starts up again behind us: "That pepper-box over there was a most interesting point strategically—"

He gets no further. Karl looks around indignantly and says firmly: "Shut your mug. . . ."

He does not say it ill-naturedly, but quietly rather, and so finally.

Then he goes forward, forth from the strategic deposition of embattlements, from the dim chattering of the groups of tourists, forth from lobster, buttered rolls, pictures of ladies and bank managerships, forth from the ten years of peace.

He goes, and his face grows ever more stern; the eyes become narrower, they scrutinize the ground; grass rustles, stones scrunch, a signboard still gives a warning of danger somewhere, but Karl troubles himself about these things no more. He is searching.

Out over the shell-pitted fields, through remnants of barbed-wire entanglements goes the track.

The interpreter lags far behind, having bawled after us a pack of cautions. Dugouts that have been buried and excavated again come to view, stick-bombs and dixies riddled with holes lie about, in the yellow clay sticks a poor rusty fork and from its end hangs half a spoon.

We go on for some time. Karl often stands still and examines the lie of the land. Then he nods and presses on. The direction of a trench is perceptible. But only the direction—craters, between which a couple of tracks thread their way and then take a sharp turn toward a corner.

A few more steps. Another look. Karl has found what he seeks.

He is silent a space before he says: "Here—" and stops—and goes on again: "Hereabouts it must have been—here we were then—everything was roaring, a couple of shots and then, 'Charge—'" He repeats: "And then, 'Charge—'"

With that he quits the trench, leaps up and himself charges. But this is no longer Karl Broeger, the man of the bank managership and the football news; this is another, ten years younger, this is Sergeant Broeger, whom the ground has laid hold on again, the wild, ashy smell of the battlefields, and remembrance that has burst upon him like a whirlwind.

His movement is no longer what it was; here is nothing more of the hesitant searching; this is not even the gait I have been accustomed to; unconsciously, involuntarily there is once again a suggestion of the dodging, intent, cautious gliding, the instinctive sureness of the beast; he is not aware himself how his head is shrunk back on his shoulders, how his arms hang loose at the joint ready for a fall, nor that he avoids exposing himself, so as not to be seen, but keeps always under cover.

So we go forward. A couple of hours ago he would perhaps have been unable to find his way at all; now he knows every fold of the ground; the past has him again. Thus we follow the track—two fellows in well-tailored suits, with hats and walking-sticks—we follow the track over which he and his platoon crawled on that terrible night, when the parachute-flares hung over the annihilation like giant arc lamps, and all the ground about Thiaumont and Fleury heaved and tossed like a sea under the fountains of explosion—we pass that way again, and about us is the boundless quiet of the evening, but in the ears of Sergeant Broeger that battle roars, he grips his walking-stick like a hand-grenade, once again he leads his men through the shell holes to the assault on the town.

And the town is no longer there. It has vanished, wiped level with the ground: never built up again, because the earth is still mined, chock full of explosives, too dangerous ever to be worked more.

Karl leans against the monument that marks the site where Fleury once stood, the village of terror, whose ruins were stormed and lost six times in one night. "This is where George was killed," says he. "He was close beside me all the time. Then when we had to retreat, he was gone. And afterwards—"

Afterwards, when they had taken the place again, they found only a piece of body, but did not know if it were he. And so he was just reported "missing," and his mother still hopes to this day that he will walk into her red-plush parlor one morning and, grown big, strong and broad, sit down beside her on the sofa.

"There is no reason why he should not still be living," reflects Karl and looks at me dimly. "Do you suppose he would have become a musician? He wanted to, then."

I do not know, and we go. The twilight has turned to dark blue. Karl stops once more and with a sweeping gesture: "Look now, I simply cannot understand it; here it was once so that a man could not think any more, Hell it was, and it was nothing but Hell, the last, and the end, a cauldron, hopeless, and a man sat in it and was a man no more—and now here we are walking about and it is just a little valley, like this, in the dark, a harmless hillock—"

The mausoleum towers white in the darkness. The touring busses prepare to leave. Humming, off they go in their upholstered rows.

The dark landscape again rolls past the car. Memorials, many memorials, slip through the light of the headlamps. On them the talk is mostly of *Gloire* and *Victoire*. Karl shakes his head: "That does not tell all the story, no, not all by any means. But they are right to put up monuments, for more was never suffered than yonder and all about. But they have left out one thing: Never again. That is missing. You—"

The road runs white ahead and now begins to rise. From behind the clouds the moon comes out red and sorrowful. Gradually it grows smaller and brighter till it shines out silver on the American cemetery at Romagne. Fourteen thousand crosses gleam in the pale light. Fourteen thousand crosses, in rows behind each other—the eyes smart, so bewilderingly straight they are, vertical, diagonal. Under each a grave. On each an inscription: Herbert C. Williams, 1st Lieut., Chemical Warfare Service, Connecticut, 13 Sept. 1918—Albert Peterson, 137 Inf., 35 Div., North Dakota, 28 Sept. 1918—fourteen thousand—twenty-five thousand there were. Killed in the attack on Montfaucon, killed a few weeks before the peace. Only one cemetery for so many. Everywhere, in scores of places, lie the others, the white wooden crosses of the French, the black ones of the Germans.

In the midst of the fourteen thousand crosses on the broad central pathway a solitary man, remote and small, goes to and fro, ever to and fro. That is more afflicting than if all were still. Karl pushes on.

In the towns children are playing in the squares. Around them are the shops, houses, churchyards, newspapers, noise, shouting, streets, the world; but they play on, engrossed in their simple games, play that is the same all the world over.

"Children," says Karl, and in the darkness one cannot see what is the matter with him, "children are the same in all places, do you see—children, as yet they do not know anything—"

And while I am still pondering upon it and glance at him, he turns upon me: "Now, get on, man—what are we standing here for?" and turns his head, and all the rest of the journey looks intently out of the window.

4

JOSEF'S WIFE

It was 1919 and the elder tree was already in flower when Corporal Josef Thiedemann came home. Only his wife was with him. She had brought him away herself—she had not taken even the coach-man with her.

The whole way the two sat side by side in silence. The gleaming brown backs of the horses before them rocked lightly to and fro. They entered the village street and passed slowly along it. Folk were standing before their houses in the evening sun and occasionally a woman would put her hand on the arm of her husband. But Thiedemann recognized no one—not even his wife or his horses.

He had been buried by a trench mortar in July, 1918, when he was sitting with a few pals in a dugout. It was only the merest chance—a piece of the broken wooden lining of the dugout thrusting obliquely across him—that saved him from being crushed. It was some hours before they could get to him and everyone believed that he must already have been suffocated; but two of the splintered beams had so interlocked that there remained a narrow chink between them through which he was still able to get a little air. That had saved his life.

≈

Thiedemann was still conscious when they got him out, and to all outward appearance practically unhurt. He sat apathetically on the ground for a time at the edge of the trench, staring absently at the dead bodies of his comrades. A stretcher-bearer shook him by the shoulder and tried to press a coffee cup with some brandy between his teeth. Then he drew a deep sigh and collapsed.

It appeared that he had suffered a severe shock, and for almost a year he passed from one nerve hospital to another. Then at last his wife had managed to get permission to bring him home.

As the coach turned into the lane leading to the farm and jolted its way across to the shed, Thiedemann straightened himself up. His wife turned pale and held her breath. There were pigs grunting in the sty and the fragrance of the linden trees drifted across. Thiedemann turned his head first this way, now that, as if in search of something. But then he sank down again and continued listless, even when his mother came in as he sat at table. He ate what was set before him and afterward made a tour of the house. He found his way everywhere, knew exactly where the cattle were kept, and where the bedroom was. But he recognized nothing. The dog, which at first had sniffed him excitedly, afterward lay down by the stove and whimpered. It did not lick his hands or jump up upon him.

≈

During the first few weeks Thiedemann sat much alone in the warm sun beside the barn. He paid no heed to anyone and was left to do as he liked. He often suffered at night from attacks of suffocation. Then he would leap up and strike out about him and scream. On one such occasion he almost bled to death as a result of having smashed the window and injured his wrist. So his wife had wire-mesh windows put in the bedroom.

Later on Thiedemann was very happy to play with the children. He would make them little paper boats and cut pipes for them from willow twigs. They were fond of him, and when huckleberry time came they took him with them to the woods to look for some. On the way home they wanted to take a short cut and go across a stretch of open country. But they had hardly left the cover of the last trees before he began to be restless. Frightened and excited, he shouted something to the children and flung himself on the ground. They looked at him in astonishment. He dragged the little one beside him down to the earth and could not be persuaded to go any farther over the open field in an upright position. He wanted to crawl and kept ducking continually. The children were at a loss to know what to do, so they set off to fetch his wife. And as they made off across the field Thiedemann cried after them in the utmost alarm and shut his eyes, as if something terrible were about to happen.

As time went on he grew fat and flabby—he did nothing and ate heedlessly and too much. He came gradually to know the people in the house; but he did not understand that he belonged to them. Their appearance was familiar to him, no more. He was almost always kindly and contented. Only now and then, if he happened to see a piece of newly split, white wood, he would cry and it was not easy to comfort him.

⁓

His wife managed the farm alone. She dismissed the foreman because at table he once mocked a certain helpless gesture of Thiedemann's. The fellow came back again a few days later to explain that he had not meant any harm, but she merely handed him his wages without listening to him and went out of the room. One evening when the miller's son had been making advances to her and had closed the door upon her, she seized a sporting gun which hung on the wall and stood there with it until he made off grinning sheepishly. Others also tried but none succeeded. The woman was thirty-five, and of a dark, grave beauty. She worked hard, but she remained alone.

During the first few months doctors often came to the farm. Thiedemann would hide from them and each time had to be searched for. Only when his wife called would he come willingly. One doctor remained at the farm almost a whole year to treat him. When he left, the woman had to sell a few head of cattle. The crops also were damaged that year by the summer rains and the potatoes had suffered as well. It was a difficult year.

But Thiedemann's condition did not change. The woman received the doctor's verdict unmoved, as if it were a matter of complete indifference to her. But at night, when Thiedemann would mutter some incomprehensible words in his sleep, tossing to and fro in his bed, she would press herself against him as if the warmth of her body must help him—and she would listen and ask and call to him. He would not answer but would become quieter and then fall quickly asleep.

So the years passed.

≈

A comrade of Thiedemann's once came to visit them for a few days. He had brought with him a few photographs from those times, and on the last evening he showed them to the woman. Among these was one group picture of Thiedemann's section. In it the men, naked to the waist, were squatting about before a dugout and grinning as they searched their shirts for lice. Thiedemann was second from the right, and smiled as he held up one hand, the thumb and forefinger tightly pressed together.

The woman looked at the pictures one after another. While she was so engaged Thiedemann entered the room. With heavy tread he walked across to the stove and sat down on a chair. The woman took up the group picture and held it a long time in her hand. Her eyes moved from the faded snapshot to the apathetic figure by the stove.

"It was there?" she asked. The friend nodded.

The woman continued silent a while. Thiedemann's heavy breathing could be heard in the stillness. A moth flew in at the window and fluttered about the lamp. The quivering shadow of its wings flickered over the table and upon the photographs and lent them an illusion of movement and life. The woman pointed to the pictures of trenches and shattered villages.

"Is it still like that?"

"Sure to be," said the comrade. With a quick movement she offered him a pencil and smoothed out a sugar bag which lay at hand on the window ledge.

"Write the name of the place. And the way."

The friend lifted his head.

"Do you want to go there?"

≈

The woman studied the picture in which Thiedemann, still smiling and well, was seated in front of the dugout. Then she looked up calmly.

"Yes," she replied.

"We should all like to go there again, once," said the friend meditatively as he slowly spelled out the letters. "You will have to pass by way of Metz."

It was a long time before all was ready. Folk did not understand why she wanted to go, and tried to dissuade her. But she heeded no argument. She set about quietly and resolutely gathering together what was necessary for the journey. When people questioned her she answered them briefly. She said simply, "It must be."

The journey was difficult. The traveling gave Thiedemann pains in his head and the woman had no one with her to help her. Neither did she understand the language. But she would merely stand and look at the people until they understood what she meant.

On the afternoon of the third day they reached the place where Thiedemann's company had been. It was a stark, drab village with long rows of gray houses. Nothing was to be seen of the ruins in the photograph. The place had been entirely rebuilt.

A couple of *chars à bancs* with tourists drew up in front of the inn. An interpreter came toward the woman and addressed her. She asked if he could tell her anything of the sector where Thiedemann had been buried. He shrugged his shoulders—it was all fields again now; it had been under cultivation some time.

"Everywhere?" asked the woman.

"Oh, no!" The interpreter began to show signs of understanding and explained that near by, hardly a mile away, the region of trenches and shell holes still lay almost exactly as it had been before. Would she like him to conduct her there?

She nodded, and, hardly taking time to deposit her baggage at the inn, they set off.

The day was clear and fine. A breeze was blowing across the slopes, and tiny blue butterflies passed fluttering among the trenches and wire entanglements. Poppies and chamomile were growing about the edges of the craters. The meadows which still intruded here and there into this landscape gradually fell behind, the village vanished and, as they passed over the summit of a ridge of hills, there rose up suddenly about them the wan silence of the battlefields, disturbed only by a few small groups of men at work here and there among the shell holes. They were the metal gatherers, explained the guide—looking for iron, copper, and steel.

"Here?" asked the woman. The guide nodded.

"The soil is crammed full of munitions," said he. "So the whole area has been farmed out to a metal-salvage company. Any bodies they find are collected and buried in the various cemeteries around." He pointed away to the right where long rows of white crosses were to be seen gleaming in the sun.

≈

The woman stayed out there with Thiedemann until evening. She went with him through many trenches and craters, she stood with him before many collapsed and broken dugouts. Often she would look at him, then always went on again. But he walked listlessly along and no light quickened in his extinguished countenance.

Next morning the woman was out there again. She knew the way now, and day after day the two were to be seen wandering slowly over the clayed fields of craters—the weary, stooping man and the big, taciturn woman. At evening they would return to the inn and go to their room.

Sometimes the interpreter would join the two on the battlefield. Once he conducted them to a region where few tourists ever came. Not a soul was to be seen except a couple of squads of salvagers at their work.

At one place the maze of front-line trenches had been left practically undisturbed. Thiedemann stopped in front of a dugout and stooped down. He had often done so before, but now the woman halted and clutched the arm of the interpreter. A few rotten boards that had lined the dugout walls were protruding from the entrance. Thiedemann explored them with his hands, gropingly, cautiously.

At that moment there sounded suddenly a sharp hammering from some salvagers starting to dig a couple hundred yards off. So intolerably loud did it seem that the woman made a gesture as if to hush it with her hand—but the next moment a heavy crash shook the ground and was followed by a whistling, howling, hissing, then a desperate, yelling cry from the group of salvagers.

"An explosion!" shouted the interpreter, running across. "They struck a shell when they were digging!"

The woman did not know how it had happened, but already she was kneeling beside a man whose leg was smashed to pieces. She had ripped the sleeve from a workman's jacket and was wrapping it round the thigh; she seized an iron staff from the ground, forced it into the knot and bound up the man who fainted as he propped on his elbows to see the wound. His mates carried him off to the huts. The woman stood up. The interpreter showered her with talk—this was the seventh explosion here in two weeks! She looked about her for a wisp of grass with which to wipe the blood from her hands. Then all at once she was alert and listening. The injured man was already out of earshot, but still a hollow, stifled crying could be heard. She ran back—

The cry was from Thiedemann. He was lying flat on the ground as if he had flung himself down madly under cover. His shoulders were heaving and he was shouting into the earth. The interpreter looked at him in astonishment and wanted to lift him up. But the woman warned him away.

A couple of workmen came running across from the hut. They imagined that Thiedemann had been wounded and wanted to carry him off. But the woman allowed no one to come near. She was suddenly transformed; she hardly moved and yet she compelled them all away, such power, and such imploring fear was in her eyes. Shaking their heads they at last went off, even the interpreter, and the woman watched them till they were lost in the maze of trenches. Then she sat down on the steps of the dugout and waited.

≈

The twilight fell and Thiedemann became still. He lay on the ground there now just as he had done then, and the notes of the Angelus bell floated over the night camp. But the woman continued to sit motionless.

At last Thiedemann stirred. He tried to lift himself on his elbows, but he sagged down again. After a while he attempted a second time. The woman gave him no help. She only withdrew deeper into the shadows of the dugout.

Thiedemann groped over the ground. His hands loosed a fragment of the timber-lining. He tried to stand up, but he could not. Then he sat and passed his hands about continually over the grass. He lifted his head and turned it slowly this way and that. And so he continued a long time.

A bird began to sing above the heads of the two people. Thiedemann's hands became still. "Anna—" said he gently, amazed.

The woman still said nothing, but now, as she took Thiedemann's arm to lead him away, her face suddenly twitched as if it would break in pieces, and for an instant she staggered.

A few weeks later Thiedemann was able to take over the farm again. His wife had managed it well; for the stock had increased by fourteen heifers and she had been able also to purchase two meadows and a couple of fields.

5

ANNETTE'S LOVE STORY

Annette Stoll grew up in a small university town in central Germany. She was a fresh, fair-complexioned little girl, light of heart and prone to laughter, attending school with moderate zeal and very fond of sweets and moving pictures. The playmate of her childhood was young Gerhard Jäger, some three years older than herself, thin and lanky, with a partiality for books and serious discussions.

They were neighbors and their parents were on friendly terms, so it came about that the two grew up as brother and sister together. The adventures of the one were the adventures of the other also—the deserted gardens, the winding lanes, the Sundays filled with pealing bells, the summer meadows, the twilight, the stars, the fragrance and breathless, dark enchantment of youth—all these they had in common.

Later on it was different. The girl, early to mature and pretty, attained to the cool self-possession of pert sixteen. She slipped suddenly out of the frank familiar garden of childish comradeship into the twilight of intriguing secrets. Young Gerhard Jäger, who had but recently been her older friend and protector of her childhood's days, now seemed to her awkward, much younger than herself, and in the irresolution of his thoughtfulness even a little ridiculous. She liked the round, smooth things of life, and there was little difficulty in forecasting her career—it would be safe and peaceful and ordinary, with a respectable husband and healthy children.

By the time Gerhard had completed his first semester at the university, the two were strangers to each other.

Then the war came. The general fever of enthusiasm infected the little town. Day by day ever more of the sixth-form boys and younger undergraduates exchanged their gay student caps for the gray regimentals of the volunteer. And their boyish faces looked a trifle remote already, more serious, older, but beautiful, too, in the readiness of their youth for the sacrifice, and yet still too near to the school bench, the rowing club and the evening escapade—too near to peace still to permit of any true understanding of what it portended and whither they were going.

Gerhard Jäger was one of the first to volunteer. The quiet, hesitant, thoughtful boy appeared transfigured. He seemed irradiated by an inward fire that was yet far removed from the extravagance of the war-intoxicated professors. He and his mates saw in the war more than mere fighting and defense; for them it was the great attack that should sweep away the outworn ideals of a smugly regulated existence and rejuvenate life grown senile.

They left all together one Sunday. The station was full of weeping, excited and enthusiastic friends and relations. Almost the entire town had turned out. There were flowers on every side, twigs of fresh green were stuck into the muzzles of the rifles, and the band was playing, and shouts and calls passed back and forth. Just as the train was leaving, Gerhard Jäger suddenly saw Annette before the window of his compartment. She was waving to someone in another carriage. He caught at her hand.

"Annette—"

≈

She laughed and threw him what still remained of her flowers.

"Bring me something pretty from Paris!"

He nodded but was able to say no more, for the train was already moving faster and the station in an uproar of song and blaring brass bands. The girl's fluttering, white summer dress was the last memory that he took away with him. . . .

During the first few months Annette heard little of Gerhard. Then letters and field post cards began to come more and more frequently. She wondered at it rather; she was at a loss to understand why it should have happened so suddenly. But even less did she understand the reason why all these letters should have preoccupied themselves—as the months went by, each more exclusively than the last—with memories of their common childhood. She looked for resounding descriptions of valiant attacks, and each time was disappointed afresh to hear only things which she knew and which bored her.

Gerhard's brigade suffered terrible losses in the battle in Flanders. A few days later his parents received no more than a short note to the effect that out of two hundred, he and twenty-seven others were still uninjured. Annette, on the other hand, had a long letter in which Gerhard recalled almost passionately a certain morning in May and the white-blossoming cherry tree behind the cathedral cloister. His father shook his head as he read the letter. He was given up to the larger ideas and would have been glad had his son shown himself a little more heroic. Annette laid the close-written letter aside with a shrug—she could not remember the May morning any more.

The surprise of the two was so much the greater when, shortly afterward, they were told that Gerhard had shown such remarkable bravery in the battle in Flanders that he had been decorated and promoted on the field.

Some time later he came home on leave, lithe, slim and sunburned, quite other than Annette had imagined from the letters. In contrast to the garrulous pride of his father he appeared doubly solemn, sometimes even absent-minded and curiously distrait. The first time that he found himself alone with Annette, after a strange, almost speechless hour of awkward staring and sudden flashes, all at once he took her by the hand and asked her if they could not be married. And he stuck to it in most persistent and silent fashion, even when it was objected that they were still too young. He was nineteen and she not yet quite seventeen.

There was nothing unusual then in hasty war marriages and betrothals—such things were of a piece with the general enthusiasm. After the first momentary surprise, Annette quickly accustomed herself to the idea—she decided it would be intriguing to be the first of her school class to be married—and she quite liked that manly young officer who had developed out of the dreamy Gerhard of her childhood—and more than that was hardly necessary. Their parents also, being well-to-do and good-natured and patriotic into the bargain, gave their consent, and were even pleased—the wedding would afford pretext for a grand party.

The ceremony was at midday. In the afternoon, during the wedding luncheon, an extra edition of the newspaper appeared, reporting a new great victory on the eastern front. Gerhard's father had every available paper brought in and read the accounts aloud to the assembly. Ten thousand Russians taken prisoner! The wedding guests gave themselves up to an orgy of rejoicing. Speeches were made, patriotic songs were sung, and to everyone Gerhard in his gray uniform appeared as the embodiment of the ideas with which they were all intoxicated.

≈

The parson shook him by the hand, the schoolmaster slapped him on the shoulder, his father incited him to wade into them again to the same purpose, and all present proceeded to drink with him to "Victory, Fame and Good Luck in Battle." Gerhard, who had become only more gloomy and taciturn, thereupon sprang up suddenly, seized his glass and, as the assembly sat round in silent expectancy, brought it down again so hard upon the table that it splintered. "You—" said he, "you—" and with dark glowering eyes looked from one to the other—"What do you know about it?" and went out.

That evening and the whole night through he talked passionately with Annette—as if he would keep something that was threatening to elude him—he spoke of youth, of purpose, of life. All the time he talked only of her—and yet it often seemed to her as if he did not mean her at all.

The next evening he went back to the Front. But the whole day he tried to spend alone with Annette. He was like a man in a fever. He wished to see no one else, but only to roam with her through the squares and gardens and to be with her in the meadows by the river until it should be time for him to depart. To her he seemed strange and she was almost a little afraid of him. As he took his farewell he held her tightly and talked quickly, stammering for haste, as if there were still much left unsaid, undone. Then he sprang into the train, which was already moving.

Four weeks later he was killed and Annette was a widow at seventeen.

The war went on and the years grew more bloody, until at last there was hardly a house in the little town where they did not wear mourning, and Annette's fate, which had at first often been talked of, paled before the harder trials of those families where both fathers and sons had fallen. And she herself soon ceased to feel it. She was too young, and the few days they had passed together had not been sufficient for her to look upon Gerhard as her husband. For her he was but one friend of her youth who had fallen—as so many others.

≈

Yet it was remarkable that a certain remoteness now entered her life. She had no real fellowship with her girl friends of before—for that she was no longer maiden enough. And she found, on the other hand, that she belonged as little to the grown-ups—for that she was still too much a maiden. And so it was that she hardly knew how she should behave. Too much had come, and gone too quickly.

But the events of the last years of the war left her no time for reflection. She worked from morning till night as a voluntary-aid nurse in a hospital. The maelstrom of the times swept in and swallowed up its individuals.

Then the Armistice came, the revolution, the time of the *putsches*, the nightmare of the inflation—and at last, when it was all over and Annette came to herself, she discovered almost with astonishment that she had grown into a woman of twenty-five without her life having increased its riches by anything more than before. For of Gerhard she now thought hardly at all.

Shortly afterward her parents died. Their wealth had so dwindled that Annette had to be thankful to get a post as hospital nurse in a North German town.

A few months later she made the acquaintance of a man who paid her many attentions and desired to marry her. She hesitated at first, but as time went on she became fond of him and the day was fixed for the wedding.

≈

She ought now to have been really happy, yet she became restless. Something within her, she knew not what, shrank from it. She would catch herself lost in a muse; she would listen absently while anyone talked to her. Her thoughts became nebulous and withdrew into the remoteness of a dim, shadowy melancholy. She would waken at night crying for no reason. Then again she would try through impetuous tenderness, through a passionate longing for affection, to escape over the strange barrier that was building up slowly before her.

Sometimes, when she was alone in her room and would look out of the window at the bare, gray houses opposite, it seemed to her that the walls dissolved into a transparent haze and doors would open beyond, and there were lanes there and gabled roofs, meadows in summer, and hot deserted gardens—and then there would overtake her a sudden imperative longing to be home again, till she came at last to believe that it was thence all her trouble came. It was just homesickness, and she needed only to go back there once more and see it again to overcome it.

She decided to revisit her home for a few days and her fiancé accompanied her.

They arrived in the evening. Annette was very excited. No sooner had she unpacked her things at the hotel than she took leave of her fiancé and went out alone.

⁓

She stood before the house that had been her home. She ran down the garden. Her excitement grew. The moon was shining and the roofs glistened. There was a smell of spring in the air and she had a sense of something near, of something about to begin—already it was rising up over the horizon, it was coming, seeking to be remembered, seeking a name.

She went out across the meadows. The grass was heavy with dew. The cherry trees gleamed like fresh snow. And all at once it was there: a voice, a remote, forgotten, buried voice; a remote, forgotten, buried face; something within lacerated, something breathless, something endlessly far, unthinkably weary, heavy, sorrowful—she had ceased to think of it; now it stood up and was mightier than it had even been in life; all at once very dear, lost, and yet never possessed—Gerhard Jäger.

She came back to the hotel, tottering, dizzy. She looked at her fiancé—how alien to her he was! She could have hated him as he stood there, alive and whole, before her. It was with difficulty that she said to him the few necessary words. He wanted to talk with her; he pleaded with her to reconsider it; he promised her to wait. She merely nodded to it all and wanted to be alone.

The few days she had been with Gerhard became now for Annette a torment and a secret. She turned out his letters and read them till her eyes were blinded with tears. She sought out some of his comrades and was tireless in asking them what they knew of him. One had talked with him a great deal and spoken to him even on the day on which he was killed. For the first time Annette heard now what the war had really been; for the first time she realized of what Gerhard had spoken to her the night before his departure; for the first time she understood what it was that he had desired of her—a resting place, a haven, a little fire of love in the midst of so much hate; one spark of humanity in the midst of annihilation; warmth, trust, a ground to stand on; the earth, a homeland, a bridge whereby to come back again.

So she became a prey to remorse, and to love. She, for whom it had all been but a little vanity, a trifling inclination for the unusual, a little friendship and a bit of girlish pleasure; she who had so quickly forgotten, who had hardly remembered it at all, now began suddenly to love—to love a shadow.

＝

She withdrew herself from everything. Her acquaintances tried to argue with her, to help her to find herself again. But it was of no avail. Had she lived with a human being it might perhaps have been possible to free her; but she lived with a memory.

She grew ever more strange. Often when alone in her room she would talk aloud to herself. Before long she had lost her post. Later she joined a small sect which held spiritual séances. Once she thought she saw Gerhard coming to her. So the years went by. . . . One day she was no more. . . . The last thing that she saw was the dark cross cast by the frame of the window behind which stood the setting sun.

6

THE STRANGE FATE OF JOHANN BARTOK

Johann Bartok, an engineer's fitter, had been five months married when the war broke out. He was called up at once and sent to join an Austrian garrison on the frontier. The day he left he was occupied putting his affairs in order and in handing over his small business to his wife and his assistant. He even succeeded in getting two additional commissions. This took him, it is true, well into the afternoon; but, on the other hand, he had the satisfaction of knowing that all would now be well until Christmas at least. When evening came he put on his best suit and went with his wife to a photographer. Hitherto they had not risen to having their photograph taken—they had had to work hard to get on, so that any such thing must have seemed to them a foolish expense. But now it was a different matter. The photographer brought the pictures to the train the next morning. Though they were rather larger in size than Bartok had expected, he tried to make a section showing both their faces fit inside the cover of his watch, but could not manage it; so he took his knife, cut away his portrait and retained only that of his wife. Now it fitted.

≈

Bartok's regiment was soon moved to the Front. It advanced during the winter of 1914 and became engaged in a fierce night skirmish, during the course of which the enemy made a flanking movement and cut off three companies. Those defended themselves for a whole day; then, having no more ammunition, they were obliged to surrender. And Bartok was one of them. The prisoners spent some months in a concentration camp. Bartok sat about in the hut the whole day and brooded. He would have liked to know how things were going with his wife, and whether she had been able to secure any fresh jobs for the firm, for that of course must now furnish her livelihood. But there was not one letter for the whole camp, and all that Bartok could do was to try to send out letters full of advice and the addresses of people at home who might perhaps be in need of a new iron gate, for example, or a water-closet. Toward the beginning of April a batch of 1,800 men was assembled and transported to the coast. Among these were Bartok and his mates. They were embarked on a steamer and a rumor went round that they were to be shipped to a camp in eastern Asia.

During the first few days they were almost all of them seasick. After that they sat about, huddled together in the stale atmosphere of the dark holds, and smoked so long as they had any cigarettes left. They could catch a glimpse of the sea only through a few narrow portholes, so they took turns looking out. The water was blue and clear, and sometimes white wings or the shadow of a large fish could be seen.

≈

Gradually the watch became careless. The prisoners observed it and conceived the plan of surprising the garrison and making themselves masters of the ship. Some of them spied out the rooms where the arms were kept, and others secretly furnished themselves with marlinspikes, ropes and knives.

Then one wet stormy night they broke loose. Three gigantic sergeants led the troop to which Bartok belonged. Seemingly innocent, they lounged toward the companionways and then suddenly threw themselves like cats upon the astonished guards, who could make no resistance. A few moments later they had broken down the hatches and were out on deck.

Part of the crew were overpowered in their sleep and the rest had to surrender. Only the captain and two officers dug themselves in and opened fire. Three prisoners were killed by revolver shots. But when a machine gun was mounted and put in position, the captain, severely wounded, surrendered.

It was the prisoners' intention to cut their way through to some neutral port, for they were well furnished with weapons and food, and there were a certain number among them who had been to sea before. A former ship's officer took command. There was drill every day and Bartok was trained as one of the gun crew. The officer in command calculated that they would need a full week to make the next port. But it turned out otherwise. For on the fourth day the low, gray hull of a man-of-war thrust forward over the sky line. With smoking funnels it headed straight for the steamer with the prisoners.

They tried to make off but were not fast enough. Then they put all in readiness to defend themselves, hoping to hold out until nightfall and then escape under cover of fog and darkness.

But they had no success. They had guns, it is true, but were unable to reach the cruiser with them. After one hour many had been killed and they were obliged to hoist the white flag. The ship's officer shot himself as the first boat from the warship came alongside. The captain of the cruiser treated the prisoners not as soldiers but as mutineers, and they were sent to an island penal settlement. A few of the ringleaders were shot, and Bartok's friend, Michael Horvath, was one of these. He handed over to Bartok his watch and his pocketbook. "Good luck, Johann," said he, shaking his hand in farewell, "might as well die this way as the other—it all comes to the same in the long run—Let's hope you get through! If my mother is still alive then, give her these things, will you?"

The remainder of the prisoners were found guilty of mutiny. Every fifth man was sentenced for life, and the rest to fifteen years' labor. When they numbered off, Bartok's luck was in—he received only fifteen years.

"Fifteen years," thought he the evening of the first day as he lay down with aching limbs in a corner of the burning, corrugated iron hut, "fifteen years. I am thirty-two today. I shall be forty-seven then." He took out the portrait of his wife from the watch case and looked at it a long time. Then he shook his head and tried to go to sleep.

The work was hard and the climate murderous. One hundred and eighty men died in the first year. In the second, one hundred and ten. The fourth year Bartok made friends with Wilczek, a farmer from the Banat region. The sixth he buried him. The seventh he lost his front teeth. In the eighth year he learned that the war had long been over. In the ninth year he turned gray. The tenth year sixteen men escaped but were captured again. The twelfth year none spoke of home any more. The world had dwindled to an island, life was toil and deep sleep, desire was quenched, pain was dulled, memory broken—over the meaningless remnant of beings that lay down dumbly each night to die and yet always rose up again in the morning, there stood, large and imperious, only guards, and fever and despair.

≈

When the warden told them they were free, they did not believe it at first. To the very last day they had counted on his coming and explaining to them that they must remain yet another five or ten years—so little could they picture to themselves what it was to be free. They packed up their few belongings and marched down to the harbor. Bartok looked about him once more. There, before the huts, he saw the survivors of those comrades who were under life sentence and who must now be left behind. They were staring after them fixedly in silence. Before leaving, Bartok had asked two of them if he could not send them something from home. "Shut your mouth!" one had replied and walked away. The other was past understanding. But the first man came running after them a few paces—"We are coming too!" he cried. The others did not move. They merely stood and stared.

On the way to the ship Bartok took out his watch. The portrait of his wife was still there—it was completely faded and nothing recognizable remained. But he took it out and tried to think back. It was a long time since he had done so, and soon his head began to swim, so unaccustomed was he to it.

Ashore, he continued in company with a couple of mates from the same district. They found that their homeland now belonged to a country which had previously been fighting against them. The district had been ceded by the treaty of peace. They did not understand, but they accepted it provisionally. For to them the whole world had changed in these fifteen years. They saw houses, streets, motor cars, men—they heard familiar names, yet all was strange. The towns had grown, the traffic worried them and they found difficulty in understanding what was going on around them. Everything moved too quickly. They were used only to think slowly.

At last Bartok reached his home town. He was obliged to walk slowly and support himself on his stick, his knees trembled so from excitement. He found the house again in which he had lived. The business was still there, but nobody knew anything of his wife. The lease had changed hands often during the last ten years. She must have left long since. Bartok hunted everywhere. He learned at last that she was now probably living in a larger town in the west.

He set off to the city the name of which had been given him. There he stood before many a door and in many a passageway and asked. When none could give him any information, and weary and hopeless he was about to go away again, he suddenly had an idea. He turned about and gave the official the name of his former assistant. The clerk looked again in the book and found him. The woman had married him seven years since. Bartok nodded. He understood now why no letters had come, why he had never heard anything from home. They had assumed that he was dead.

Slowly he mounted the stairs and rang the bell. A child of five years opened the door. Then his wife came. He looked at her, uncertain whether it were she, not trusting himself to speak. "I am Johann," he said at last.

"Johann!" She took one step and sat down heavily in a chair. "Holy Mother!" She began to weep. "But we had a notice, then—a certificate—you were dead!"

She pulled open a drawer and began rummaging in it with trembling hands, as though her very life hung upon finding the notice again.

"Yes, yes, never mind"—Bartok moved with an absent look through the kitchen. "Is that your child?" he asked. The woman nodded. "Have you others?"

"Two—"

"So, two—" he repeated mechanically. Then he sat down on the sofa and stared ahead.

≈

"What will happen now, Johann?" the woman asked in tears. Bartok lifted his eyes.

In front of him on a low chest stood a small photograph in a gilt frame. It was the one they had had taken before he became a soldier. He took it down and considered it a long time. Then he looked again at his wife. He passed his hand over his forehead.

"Five months, wasn't it?"

"Yes, Johann—"

"And now?"

"Seven years," she answered softly. He nodded and stood up. The woman held him. "You are not going away?"

"Yes—" said he, taking up his cap.

"Stay at least until supper-time," she begged. "Till Alfred comes—"

He shook his head. "No, no—it is better so. Then you must put matters straight. It will be all right, though."

Outside before the house he stood still a while. Then he went back to the railway station and returned to his home town. There he intended to look for work and to start again.

7

ON THE ROAD

After I had lived for four days on green plums I fainted. My stomach was like glowing iron and the country road heaved before my eyes. I knew that it was bright midday and that the sun was blazing down, but everything looked gray as ashes and my knees were as weak as though I were wading through a swamp. I staggered away from the road and gave up. I lay down under a pine tree, unbuttoned my shirt and felt myself sink into a black abyss. I thought I was done for.

When I came to, it was evening. A farmer was standing beside me, shaking me. I felt that my face was wet. With my tongue I licked the drops from my lips. They burned. It was brandy. He held the bottle to my mouth. I raised myself and took a swallow. Then I shook my head—I couldn't drink any more. Even that one swallow went to my head.

The farmer was on his way home to the village where he lived. His horse was snorting and stamping in front of a covered wagon at the edge of the road. A lantern swung between the wheels. In the twilight the yellow shine of the lantern, the warm smell of the horse, the great dark figure of the man—all that was like home and it made me weak. I bit my lip and straightened myself up.

$\approx$

The farmer asked what was the matter with me. I told him that I was unemployed and that a week before, while I was on the road, someone had stolen the last of my money. He took two raw eggs out of his wagon, broke them, added some brandy and gave the mixture to me. I drank it slowly. Then I ate some of the bread that he took from his pocket. He wanted me to go along with him. I asked whether he could give me work. He said no. What could I do? Anything, I said, that didn't take long to learn. He thought for a minute and then told me that nearby there was a gang at work on the railroad. He had heard that the foreman intended to hire a couple more men—but probably the work would be too heavy for me. I said that when I had rested for a while I could handle it. I would try next day; he could just leave me where I was. He told me where to go. It was only three miles away. Then he laid some more eggs beside me, a whole loaf of bread and a sausage. I had nothing to give him in return except a small pocketknife. He didn't want to take it, but finally he did—probably he realized why I wished it. As he was leaving he gave me, in addition, an old horse blanket.

I hid the eggs under some moss. The bread and sausage I kept close beside me under the blanket. Several times during the night I woke up and reached over to touch them. I could feel, too, the rough edge of the blanket scratching my neck and smell the odor of horses. After that things weren't so bad.

As soon as it was light I dragged myself away from the edge of the road. I was worried about my possessions. In the woods I found a little clearing through which a stream flowed. I stayed there.

I was tormented by hunger now—much worse than in the last two days. But I made a careful division of my supplies. I couldn't run the risk of my stomach's rejecting so much as a mouthful; I needed every crumb to gain strength for the job. The first day I ate very little and remained in the shade. By the second day I was feeling fine; I bathed and lay for a while in the sun, being careful not to get my head in it. Despite my fear that the jobs might be taken before I got there, I spent the third day, too, in the clearing and slept and ate until there was nothing left to eat.

Next morning, I went to the railroad. The foreman looked at me doubtfully; but I was in luck: two workmen had been reported sick. He hired me.

~

There were about twenty of us and we lived in a corrugated-iron barracks near the tracks. The first morning I worked like mad, for I saw that the foreman was watching me. By noon I could hardly move and was so exhausted that I ate very little. I was in despair, for I knew that I should soon collapse. I could expect no sympathy. Already one of the workmen, a brawny black dog whom the others called Meck, had taken a dislike to me and showed it. He struck with his pick in such a way that stones kept hitting me on the shins and he made constant references to fine people who thought they were too good for their jobs—they could go to the devil.

It was oppressively hot. The corrugated-iron barracks glowed and our bare backs glistened with sweat. The rails flashed in the sun. The fellow who worked beside me was as strong as a horse and swarthy, with a wild growth of hair around his mouth. He said nothing but now and then he glanced over at me—he noticed how awkward I was. Finally, I had to stop. My hands were trembling. The hot sweat on my forehead suddenly turned cold. Then with a grunt he pushed me aside, took my pick and showed me how to do the required work with less effort. "Thanks," I said. "Mug," he answered, not unkindly. I went at it again. The day was endless; but now I knew that I could last it out.

≈

That evening I went to the foreman and got two marks advance. In the canteen I bought a package of cigarettes. The man who had helped me was sitting on a tree stump beside the barracks. His name was Heinrich Thiess. I pretended I was coming that way by accident, lighted a cigarette and offered him one. "No, thanks," he said, and spat. Brown. He preferred to chew. I went back to the foreman and traded a couple of cigarettes for a piece of chewing tobacco. An hour later I took this to him.

"It's the thin, dark kind," I said, "flavored with rum."

"You know something about it?" he asked, and took it.

"A little," I said. "But I don't like it—"

"Yes, that takes time," Thiess said.

From then on we ate together in the evening. Sometimes he caught fish in the river and we broiled them on a stick over a fire. He understood all about that sort of thing. Once he baked a hedgehog in clay. He said the gypsies considered it a holiday dish. It tasted strange, but not bad. It would have tasted better if I hadn't known it was a hedgehog. Once when I was a soldier I ate a cat without knowing it. It tasted fine.

In the evenings when we were through eating, Heinrich used to tell me about his wanderings. He was a vagabond and never worked long in one place. Those were wonderful nights. The air was warm, with a strong scent of flowers, much stronger than by day. Near our barracks there was a garden that belonged to a watchman on the railroad—one of those pathetic little farmers' gardens that you see constantly from the windows of a train. The garden was full of roses in bloom. Their fragrance often blew over to us. Then Heinrich would stand up, sniff the air and wander up and down, his head sunk, big and restive.

He would look over at the railroad watchman's house. The sickly watchman lived there with his wife. She used to sing as she washed her windows in the morning. She was much younger than he. She was healthy and pretty. Heinrich Thiess weighed one hundred and eighty pounds. He hadn't an ounce of fat.

≈

The black dog, Meck, wouldn't let me alone. He threw a shovel on my foot so that it hurt for two days afterward. He upset my lunch pail. He quarreled with me whenever he could. In the beginning Heinrich Thiess growled at him a couple of times; but Meck wouldn't let up. He hated me, although I tried to keep out of his way. "It's no good," Heinrich said, finally, "you'll have to fight it out with him. I could do it for you, but that wouldn't help. After that you'd have the whole gang on your neck. Come along."

We went into the woods and there Heinrich showed me what I had to do. "His head is hard, I know that," he said, "but his stomach is like butter. You've got to hit him in the stomach and knock his wind out."

At that time there were constant fistfights in the barracks—either between the workmen or with the farmer boys from the village. Many of us were crazy for women; every Sunday there was a fight. Heinrich had observed Meck carefully. "He'll duck down and come at you from below," he said. "Then you must kick him off and when he straightens up go at him."

We practiced every evening. "Go right ahead and hit," Heinrich said; "I can stand it." He showed me his stomach muscles. When he tightened them they were like iron.

≈

I waited a week longer. Then one Sunday it happened. There was a tense atmosphere in the barracks. Meck was beside himself. A girl he had been hanging around had sent him away. All afternoon he had been spoiling for a fight. When I came in he started to take it out on me. He expected me to be quiet as usual, but this time I wasn't quiet. "Shut your face, you dirty dog!" I told him.

Immediately the barracks became silent. Meck came at me, stooping a little, his brows drawn together, his mouth half open. You could see his joy at finally having a chance to finish me up. "What?" he said, glowering. "What was that you said, you punk?"

At one glance I took in the faces in the barracks in the half light of evening. Some were indifferent, some surprised—but in most of them was the cold, hungry expectancy of seeing someone beaten. But

I saw, too, the face of Heinrich Thiess. "I told you to keep your dirty face shut!" I roared at Meck.

The roaring was Heinrich's idea. It served its purpose. Meck was startled for an instant before he sprang at me. He hit me on the shoulder, I hit him on the neck. Then he dived to catch me around the knees, just as Heinrich had said. It happened so fast that I should have been done for if I hadn't known in advance. I jumped back and kicked. He straightened up, wavering a little, and I hit him in the stomach before he could get his arms down. He fell gasping to the floor and lay there. "He's had enough!" someone shouted from the corner. "Let him be."

I looked over at Heinrich. He nodded. I saw the circle of faces around me, I saw the gray sacks of straw, the picks and shovels on the wall; through the window I saw the warm late-afternoon sunlight on the meadow as though for the first time—and I realized suddenly that I was shaking. Now Meck could have pounded me to a jelly.

I went over to Heinrich. Suddenly there was a hoarse shout: "Look out!" I jumped aside, the next instant Heinrich sprang up and by me: a blow, a grating sound—Meck was on his knees, a knife in his hand. "Damnation!" shouted the man who had warned me. "Stabbing—he can't get away with that."

Heinrich went at him. He struck like a trip-hammer. It was terrible. The barracks groaned. He went on striking. For some time, Meck had been lying on the floor. I couldn't watch it any longer. "Leave him alone," I said. He looked at me as though he didn't know me and shook his head. "Beat it. This is something you don't understand." None of the others moved.

Later I heard that it had been done, not on my account, but on account of the knife. Heinrich was the strongest man in the barracks, and that gave him certain rights and duties which everyone recognized. Just as he could not help me out in a man-to-man fight, so he could not leave unpunished an attack from behind with a knife.

August came. Heinrich and I no longer slept in the suffocating barracks. We had taken our straw sacks out and lay in the open air. Those were unforgettable nights. The rails gleamed in the moonlight. Sometimes a train rushed by with lights and green flares. The stars sparkled, and I have never seen the heavens so vast as over that plain. The ghostly light of the Milky Way streamed over us like the smoke of a giant ship that has disappeared over the horizon.

~

Sometimes when I awoke the stars had wandered—the heavens seemed distorted—the Great Bear had crawled to his feet, and Orion stood on the other side. Then I had the feeling of the earth flying alone through space, silently dwindling beneath me to the size of a ball, and flying in an endless curve in the direction of the horizon into the abyss of the void. So tangible was this vision that I often believed I had to hold myself in place. Then when I had shaken off the dream, I would see that Heinrich Thiess was no longer lying beside me. Often I would sit for a long time staring at the dark woods which swam in the plain like cows in a misty meadow. Toward morning, when the dew fell, sudden and heavy so that it woke you up again, I would sometimes hear Heinrich come back. I knew where he had come from—from the watchman's house where the woman was. I used to pretend I was asleep when he lay down.

Then one evening the watchman was there. I was sitting with Heinrich beside a fire we had made. He was cooking a trout he had caught. The watchman sat down beside us. He was white and sweating. Heinrich acted as though he didn't notice him. The watchman talked about the weather and the heat. Heinrich said nothing. I looked at him. He was apparently undisturbed, but he fussed unnecessarily around the fire. "I'll be right back," I said.

Later I heard what had happened. The watchman told Heinrich that he had been wounded in the lungs during the war.

"Where?" Heinrich asked.

"Arras."

"I was there too," Heinrich said.

The watchman had tuberculosis. He produced a certificate from a doctor which he had brought with him. Heinrich refused to look at it. Quietly and with no appeal for sympathy, the watchman said that he hadn't much longer to live. He said, too, that he had nothing in the world besides his wife. He knew well enough that he was too sick for her. But it couldn't last much longer now, and after all, he had nothing else. . . . Could Heinrich understand that? "Yes," said Thiess. The watchman didn't say much after that. He waited for Heinrich's answer.

⟳

There was a period of silence. Heinrich stared into the fire. Then he asked again, "Where were you wounded, comrade? At Arras?" The watchman nodded. Heinrich continued to stare into the fire. He hadn't really heard even his own question.

A twig snapped in the blaze. Heinrich looked up. "Ah, yes," he said, as though he had forgotten everything. He looked at the watchman. "But I'll put it up to her myself."

"Good," said the watchman, and got up.

The following night Heinrich came back sooner than I had expected. The Warsaw-Paris Express was just thundering by. The locomotive was a fountain of sparks. Heinrich threw himself on the grass. "I'm shoving off tomorrow, Paul," he said.

I was silent. I had known it would turn out like this. But just the same it hit me so hard I couldn't say anything. "It's about time, anyway," Heinrich said after a while. "I've been too long in one spot."

"Have you told her?" I asked.

"Yes."

I looked down at the misty meadows. "It won't be much help to the fellow down there when you're gone, Heinrich. She will sit around and howl—"

"No," Heinrich said.

I looked at him. He turned over abruptly. "She's had enough of me," he said. "I told her I was married. Wanted to go home. To my wife—"

I nodded.

"She didn't howl any more after that," he said. "She was wild. Rage, you understand? Rage! That'll help her through. She has character, man—damnation!"

We were silent. "Are you really married?" I asked after a while.

"Oh, what chance—" Heinrich said, and pulled up a handful of grass.

≈

Next morning, he left. "I'll go a little way with you," I said. He shook his head. "Don't. It's better this way—"

It was very clear outside. You could see a long way. "You'll have to look out for Meck," Heinrich said. "You'd better take my sleeping place in the corner. But I don't think he'll make any trouble."

"I don't think so, either," I said.

"Well, then, good luck, Paul."

"Good luck, Heinrich."

I stayed in front of the barracks until he was beyond the woods. He didn't look back.

Three weeks later I, too, moved on.

8

I DREAMT LAST NIGHT

The red-brick hospital building lay buried deep in snow; wind rattled the window-panes; the pallid light of the lamps gleamed along the corridors; in the radiator-pipes the water knocked; and beside me in the room, his wounded back propped up by a pile of pillows, non-commissioned officer Gerhart Brockman had been dying uninterruptedly for weeks.

In the old days, before the war, he had been the teacher in a little village on the heath. While he could still speak, he often talked about it. There were four of us in the room at that time, and Brockman still believed he would be cured in a few months and released from the service. Then he would go back to the humble school beside the old village cemetery, where the bees hummed and the butterflies sat like military decorations on the tombstones—back to the path through the beechwood in the bright summer twilight—back to his teacher's room with its piano and the many books in the cases—back to that whole peaceful world of former times.

"And then, boys," he would say, and raise himself on his elbows so that the gray sleeves of his shirt fell back from his thin forearms, "the singing lesson! That was the best of all. We had a song—we could even sing it in three-part harmony; whether you believe it or not, a primary school with only one class, but we sang it in three-part harmony like a glee club. I don't know whether you know the song—'I dreamt last night—' That's something I want to hear again sometime—"

When he said that, it was hard to look without flinching into his glowing beseeching eyes. The song must have meant a great deal to him, for he returned to it often; perhaps he had sung it once to a girl he loved. Even later on, when Peterson and Fischer had died, he kept trying to talk about it; and when I hurriedly said, "Yes, I know the song, Gerhart—all the stanzas, in fact," he would wait until the floor nurse came, so that he could tell her about it. Sometimes he tried to sing her the melody in his hoarse, cracked voice. Then it seemed as though it were not a voice at all—as though it were only his last thoughts, which buzzed around each other in his skull, visible now under the tightly stretched skin, like weary flies under the glass shade of a lamp. Thirty years old, he was—Gerhart Brockman, non-commissioned officer—with a bullet lodged in his lungs, and tuberculosis of the lungs; he looked as though he were eighty.

December nights of 1917! In October, when the leaves were falling, the dying started. There had been four of us at that time, and now Brockman and I were alone in the room. The snowflakes ticked against the window like an invisible clock;

doors kept opening and closing; death tiptoed about the house; fever crept out of the corners; and sleep would not come. But when at last it did come, bringing heavy dreams, I would start suddenly awake, at the low, laborious voice from the corner of the room, a voice that whispered, cracking with horror: "Light—light—for God's sake—" Then the glow from the lamp on the table would be reflected in Brockman's eyes, which gleamed dark and uncanny in his empty face, and peered about the room, wonderingly, as though seeking some one. He never wanted to sleep; he thought that way he could not die. . . .

Christmas dawned gray and melancholy. The nurses had arranged a distribution of presents in the big hall of the hospital. There was a tree decorated with lights, tinsel and glass balls; and each of us received apples, cookies, cigarettes and even a pair of socks. At noon a caller came to see me. It was my friend Ludwig Breyer. We had lost track of each other during the offensive in Flanders, and I had heard that he had fallen. Now he stood before me safe and sound, and on his way home for two weeks' leave. But despite that, I couldn't feel any real happiness—for since Christmas eve there was no doubt left; it was about all over with Brockman.

The office had tried in vain to find relatives of his who could be summoned by telegram, so that some one at least would be with him during his last days. The attempt had failed. His parents were dead; he had no brothers or sisters; and to other questions, he now paid hardly any heed. There was a rattling in his throat all day. . . .

Ludwig Breyer stayed with me until it was getting dark. Then he had to go. He wanted to get away, too—home, to his mother.

"Don't be angry," he said pleadingly. "I'm not used to this sort of thing. In an attack, well and good—then things happen fast, and you don't see so clearly. But this, this sort of thing, gets you in the guts worse than when a regiment runs into a couple of dozen machine-guns."

131

I nodded, and watched him go until I could no longer make him out through the window. Then I lighted the lamp, although I knew that when the nurse came, she would scold me, for light had to be economized, and it was really too early. To be sure, I could hobble about, and might have gone into another room among the less seriously wounded; but I didn't want to leave Brockman alone. And at the same time I didn't want to be alone with him in the dark: even as it was, I couldn't help thinking constantly of the others that had died there. And so I lay down on the bed with my clothes on. I found the rattling easier to bear when I was lying down. There was less difference between us then. . . .

The floor nurse came into the room earlier than usual that evening. I started hastily to reach for the lamp, but she paid no attention to it. Instead she went to Brockman's bed and bent over him. She listened awhile, and then shrugged her shoulders. In the doorway appeared the pale, thin face of the operating-room nurse.

I couldn't understand what was going on. It was impossible that they intended to operate on Gerhart now!

Hurriedly I sat up on the bed. The operating-room nurse smiled at me. That made me uneasy, for when she smiled, something dangerous usually followed. Perhaps she had her eye on me too, and intended to take me once more to the butcher's block.

But like the other nurse, she went straight over to Brockman. Then she turned round. "We can try it—" she said. . . .

Astounded, I got to my feet. Outside the door in the shadowy corridor, a throng of children crowded. A young girl was with them. "She's the teacher," the nurse whispered to me. "For a week she has been in bed over there in the women's section. We told her about Brockman. And today she asked her class to come here—so that he could have some pleasure on Christmas. I hope he hears it—"

"What?" I said, and a premonition made my breath catch.

Before she could answer, the clear voices of the children rose in song: "I dreamt last night a heavy dream—"

It was as though I had received a blow. It simply overcame me. That they had thought of that! It seemed to me in that dimly lighted room—where the sweetish odor of death was already perceptible—as though a lost homeland were taking shape and coming forward to greet us. It made me choke. But I pulled myself together, and looked over at Brockman to see if he heard it too.

During the first stanza he lay motionless. The nurse beckoned to the children, and they came closer, into the frameway of the door. They began the second stanza.

Brockman's hands started to glide back and forth on the coverlid in a circular motion, like mice. Then they opened and lay flat as though in surrender. I had just decided it was the end, when he opened his eyes. They were soft, large and filled with an indescribable expression. His face was a volcanic landscape, rigid, ravaged, gray—but his eyes were more beautiful than the eyes of the girl who was singing with the children. In them was the peace that had not yet possessed his face.

The song ended. Brockman did not move. He lay quite still. The teacher nodded, and they began again. Then Brockman turned his head as though he were listening, and something like a faint, irresolute smile passed over his face. His lips moved. I bent low over him. At first I could not understand him, and I pushed his pillows a little higher.

"In three-part harmony—" he whispered, "—three-part—"

Then he stopped speaking and looked at the girl. She was very young, and I found it hard to believe that she was already a teacher. I was just nineteen myself, but by comparison I was an old man. She seemed still a child, and surely she didn't know what was happening here. Very likely she simply wanted to do a sick man a good turn, and probably had no idea that a human being, whose world was dissolving, saw his youth once more in her. . . .

At nine o'clock in the evening Gerhart was restless. At nine-thirty it was evident that his body was throwing its last reserves into the fight. At ten he was working like a locomotive; sweat streamed over his face; he shivered and gasped; his lungs rattled, and his twisted mouth snapped for air. He was slowly smothering—but he was still conscious.

"Give him morphine, nurse, so that he will have peace at once," I begged.

She shook her head. "It is against our creed," she answered.

"Then give it to me," I said, "in simple charity! Just leave it here. Forget it when you go out."

She looked at me. "Death is God's affair," she said, and added in a whisper: "If that were not so— how could one bear to be here?"

At ten-thirty it was so bad I could no longer look on. I had to do something, and suddenly I realized what it was.

How I got out of the room I no longer remember, nor how I discovered in which room the girl was. Luckily no one saw me on the way. What I said at the door I no longer recall, but the girl must have understood, for she came with me without questioning.

She knelt by Brockman's bed and lifted his damp hands. I saw her shudder as she did it, but she did not draw back. And the thing that I scarcely still hoped for—now that she was there—happened: Gerhart became quieter. To be sure, the rattle in his throat continued, but no longer so painfully. . . .

At twelve the night nurse came in. She was fat, and the only one of the nurses whom everyone hated. She recoiled a step when she saw the girl. I attempted to explain it all to her. But she only shook her head. The hospital was Catholic, and these things were taken very seriously. For the nurse, it was an everyday occurrence for some one to die; it was much more startling in her eyes that a girl should be with us during the night. "The young woman cannot remain," she said, and glared at me.

"But——" I said, and motioned toward the bed.

"He's quiet enough," she pronounced impatiently. "The young woman must go! At once! She isn't a relative."

The girl blushed. She let go his hands and started to get up. But a gurgling sound came from Gerhart's lips, his face was contorted with terror and—as I later believed—he cried: "Anna!"

"Stay here," I said wildly, and placed myself between the girl and the nurse. Now it did not matter to me what happened.

The nurse quivered with indignation. She faced the girl. "Leave the room, young woman. I myself will stay with the patient."

"That's not necessary," I asserted roughly. "He has been plagued by you often enough as it is."

She shot to the door. "Then I must report this affair. I am going to the director at once."

"Go to the devil, old night-owl!" I shouted after her.

Tense and excited, I waited to see what would happen next. I was determined not to let anyone else in. This was a matter between Gerhart and me. No one else had anything to do with it.

But, by the same token, no one else came. . . .

Gerhart died on the morning of the day after Christmas. He died easily, and at the end passed over in his sleep. The girl stayed with him until it was over. Afterward we went silently through the corridor in the pale light reflected from the snow. Now that it was all over, the dispute with the nurse lay on my conscience. The hospital was strict and intolerant in these matters. To me, it made no difference; but it might well be that the girl would be forced to leave.

"I hope you won't get too severe a punishment," I said, feeling oppressed.

She made an abrupt gesture, and looked straight at me.

"After all, that doesn't matter; on the contrary—"

I looked at her. Her face had changed completely. The evening before, when she was with her class, it had been the face of a girl—now it was the earnest, composed face of a human being who knows much and is acquainted with sorrow.

I thought of it again and again, as I went back alone, and it was a curious thing; now as the bells began to ring for early mass, I experienced, for the first time since I had become a soldier, a feeling of peace; I recognized that something had been completed, and that it was good; I knew once more that beyond and above war and destruction there was something else, and that it would return again. Quiet and confident, I went back to my room, which was filled with the gray and gold of the early light. Over there on the bed lay, not the contingent soldier Gerhart Brockman; there lay the eternal comrade. And his death was no longer a horror—it was a testament and a promise. Comforted and secure, I lay down beside him.

ABOUT THE AUTHOR

Erich Maria Remarque (1898–1970) was a German American novelist. He was the author of numerous plays, short stories, and novels, most notably *All Quiet on the Western Front.*

All photographs are from the Library of Congress Prints and Photographs Online Catalog, unless noted otherwise.

Page i: Austro-Hungarian soldiers and their sweethearts, November 30, 1915, LC-DIG-ds-00227.

Pages ii and iii: Solitary sentinel wearing pickelhaube helmet standing next to bunker, November 17, 1915, LC-DIG-ds-00228.

Pages iv and v: No mans land, Flanders Field, France, 1919, LC-DIG-ds-07411.

Pages vi and vii: Lens, France, devastated coal mining region of northern France, 1919, LC-USZ62-130599.

Page viii: Remarque in 1928, Wikipedia Commons.

Page xlix: Helmeted German soldiers lined up for review, LC-DIG-stereo-1s04001.

Page 1: At the front, (Detail), one soldier who is not wearing a gas mask grasps his throat as he falls to the ground; it is unclear if he is responding to the gas or if he has been hit by a bullet, his rifle and helmet are on the ground and his gas mask hangs against his chest, LC-USZ62-39192.

Page 19: Four de Paris in the Argonne, on the left of the American lines [1918?], LOT 6944 no. 38.

Page 35: Fort Pompelle near Reims, France [photographed between 1914 and 1918], LC-DIG-stereo-1s04088.

Page 51: German soldier's "Auf Wiedersehen" January 27, 1915. LC-B2-3357-7.

Page 71: Young couple looking lovingly into each other's eyes, c1915, LC-USZ62-38033.

Page 89: Watch: goldene Taschenuhr mit Sprungdeckel und Initialien um 1900; young woman in 1915; iStockphoto.com.

Page 105: Anti-tank barrier, made of reinforced concrete posts & heavy cables, in front of German lines, between Etain & Verdun, 1919, LOT 6944 no. 41.

Page 125: Nursing wounded near Berlin, c1914–1915, LC-B2-3540-5 [P&P].

Page 141: Remarque as a young soldier, www.remarque.uni-osnabrueck.de/.